CROWN
OF
SORROWS

CROWN OF SORROWS

HEAVY IS THE HEAD...

Bex Gil

To my brothers and sisters who struggle with chronic pain and mental illness, you are seen, your pain is real, and so is your bravery for fighting the invisible daily battles. And for those who have given up their fight—rest well—may we meet again.

CONTENT WARNINGS

This book contains mild cursing, violence, self-harm, and suicidal ideation.

SA
Nora
MANCHUR
Bataar
EBOC
Nabo
Naku Lake
Sea of Dobo
PERCIA
Terran
Sult Sea

GO
N
NW
NE
W
E
SW
SE
S
Pardus
Xian River
Gwanji
Sea of Helios
RACOUR
Baga Lake
obi
Dubali
Indo-Racour Strait
INDO

BAHM & SOL
DRYDEN

CHAPTER ONE

Valine

The nightmares returned. **Or**, more accurately, they never really left. Pain was my only companion, a loyal, yet unwanted follower. Despite the people surrounding me, I felt alone. Something was missing. *Someone* was missing. It had been a month since my husband was taken, a gaping hole in my heart a constant declaration of his absence. The birds that chirped and the flowers that were in full bloom seemed to mock me. How dare they continue on, live on, when my own life was so tragic, so hard? I glared at one robin in particular, wishing I could shoot it down with an arrow, but the bird wasn't the problem. I was.

I had a crown, combat skills, and magic, yet it wasn't enough. *I* wasn't enough to keep my husband safe. My own king who had placed my coronation crown on my head had betrayed me, and I felt fated to share the same end as my mother who had been murdered by her subservient king. I picked the petals off of a ruby-red flower in a futile attempt to take out my frustrations.

Zasper sat nearby, my back turned to her as I had no desire to talk with her. She had been urging me the past week to return to the capital, stating how fruitless our efforts were, insisting that our time would be better spent back at the palace. She wanted me to focus on governing my kingdom and to delegate the search for Lux to my soldiers. But how could I sit on my throne when one of the most important people who helped me gain it was gone?

We had spent days traveling and questioning the citizens of villages and cities, yet we had come up with no answers. No one seemed to know anything about a pale man named Noctis, who had powerful magic and showed up in my throne room only to kill his strange sister who had muttered even stranger words. Even just the thought of him sent chills crawling like bugs along my skin. No one saw the former Crown Prince Lux either—as if they'd vanished into thin air.

Although I was upset with Zasper, perhaps she was right. Our time might be better suited to consolidating resources, and I could also interrogate Dumas Stallian, my oath-sworn king who had been the one to hand my Prince Consort over to Noctis. The lesson I had taught Lux about vengeance being a disease that harmed its host was long forgotten. Once more I was consumed with rage and thoughts of revenge, the icy urge pounding in tandem to my throbbing head. I wanted to make Dumas hurt, to beg for mercy, to force him to comprehend the pain he inflicted upon me when he threw away my consort. *My husband.*

My marriage to Lux had been forced, arranged by his vile father, but our love was our choice. He was light to me, despite the darkness in which he was raised, but he was *gone.* Everything seemed a little more dull, a little more bland without him. I couldn't be sure if I would ever see him again. Although I'd expressed the sentiment in other ways, right now, I mourned the loss of the opportunity to say those words. *I love you, Lux.*

My thoughts turned towards The Creator. How could a divine entity, all-knowing and all-powerful, be truly loving when He allowed such tragedies to continually plague my life? I never doubted His existence, that fact was determined, but I did doubt His goodness. How was any of this *good*? Despite my frustrations and doubts, I prayed, *Please watch over Lux wherever he is. Help me find him. Give me wisdom and discernment. I don't know what to do.*

A voice interrupted my prayer, and I dropped the now ice encrusted flower to the ground.

"Your Majesty," Citadel said as he approached, his brows furrowed and lips ever so slightly downturned. "I feel the need to bring to your attention the state of your men. This feels like a war campaign, driving us this hard every day and night."

My eyes filled with a burning cold, my words matching in hardness. "Is my consort not deserving enough for such an effort?"

Citadel sighed, his eyes closing for a moment before responding, "Your command will be carried out, but please don't ignore the others suffering because of your own."

Indignance flashed like a blacksmith's fire, but as I looked around our encampment in which Zasper, Dryden, and the handful of soldiers that accompanied me all sat around, the clear exhaustion and despondency written on their faces was so obvious that I was a fool not to have noticed sooner. The irritation cooled and dissipated as I turned back to Citadel, the bags under his eyes suddenly more apparent. We had barely rested since we began our search, and the lack of evidence only lowered our morale. Out of the corner of my eye was Zasper, who having heard Citadel's question, stared at me expectantly.

I sighed, my shoulders crumpling. "We return to the palace."

We made haste towards Pardus, the willow and dove trees giving way to pines and ginkgoes. The capital was only a few days' hard ride away, and my entourage was eager to return. We made good time, although it was at our horses' expense, their legs trembling and nostrils flaring from the exertion. Dryden was also fatigued since running long distances was unusual for an ice leopard; short bursts of sprints or jumping were more suited for their powerful hind legs.

I berated myself for being so inconsiderate. "Let's make camp early tonight," I hollered to the group.

At least it was our last time sleeping outdoors before we reached the castle—of that I was thankful.

It was nearing the end of spring, and Dryden's pelt was starting to shed its winter coat. I brushed my hands through his fur—his dark gray spots nearly black, appearing as if ash had snowed down upon the lighter gray hair—helping to expedite the process. I pinched a clump of ashy fur between my thumb and forefinger, rubbing it together until the summer breeze took it, the hairs drifting away in indifference.

I know we need to return to the castle and rest. But how can I allow myself the time to recuperate when Lux is out there going through who knows what?

The big cat licked his paws, tongue brushing against the swollen pads underneath. *We will find him.*

If it were that easy we would have found him by now, I scoffed.

Dryden's ears flicked. *He has fire magic, so I am sure he will be fine.*

I shook my head. *You saw him for yourself. Noctis was fast and powerful. He could have killed me before you or I could do anything about it. You saw how quickly he was able to move, fast as the wind. He killed his sister or whatever she was without laying a hand on her. He was toying with us.*

Dryden growled, the vibrations seeping into my hands, *He will never get the chance to get that close to you again.*

I tugged a chunk of hair. *Your confidence is admirable, but I am afraid the enemy we face this time is far greater than Vukan. At least with him, I knew what he was, what he was capable of, but Noctis... I have no idea what he is. And Lux, is he even alive? What are they doing to him?*

Dryden paused his grooming, turquoise eyes peering into mine. *You know I am with you until the end. We will find your mate.*

His head tilted down, and I leaned in, our foreheads pressed together, his fur tickling my face.

Until the end.

As I pulled away, I couldn't help but wince as I caught sight of his pads. The centers were red and beginning to crack when they should be black. *I'm sorry. I've been so consumed with Lux that I didn't take care of everyone else.*

Dryden shook his pelt, fur flying away like a dandelion. *I understand. He is your mate. You would make a good leopard. Such loyalty is integral to our kind.*

My fingers combed through his coat as I replied, *What if my loyalty to Lux conflicts with my loyalty to my kingdom, to my people? What if I am forced to choose between the two?*

He said nothing for a moment, eyes staring off into the distance, but finally he answered, *I would choose you over my clan as Tagon did.*

But you were just a member, not the Glavnyy. I am queen, not a commoner's wife. There are people who depend on me.

The leopard shifted, whiskers twitching. *I don't know what the right answer is.*

I scoffed, *That's a first.*

Dryden glared at me, baring his teeth to expose their sharp edges, but he didn't say anything else. He must have sensed how worried and tired I was. Thankfully, exhaustion lulled me into a deep sleep, free from the nightmares where my friends died or Lux was tortured in front me.

CHAPTER TWO

VALINE

B_y the next afternoon,_ we arrived at the castle, dread clutching my insides and twisting my stomach into knots knowing I would have to make a decision. Did my responsibility lay with the search for Lux or the duty of governing my kingdom? If I said such thoughts aloud, I'd sound ungrateful. Who didn't dream of being a ruler? In fact, many people would gladly take on this position, lured by the wealth and power it promised, but the reality of the heavy responsibility was far less glamorous. I loathed that I was going to be forced to make sacrifices again—that I worked so hard for my throne and had barely sat on it.

As the hooves clattered to a halt in the castle courtyard, a familiar face appeared. The former pirate lord turned king normally wore a jovial expression, but now his face was somber, no smirk or sparkles in his eyes. He took in our group, the glaring absence of the consort deafening. "No luck, huh?"

I dismounted my gray gelding, shaking my head while avoiding his gaze, my face tucked into Tempest's flank, unable to speak for fear that the tears of frustration would spill out. I couldn't let the palace see me like that. I was just a month into my reign, and I had to solidify the people's trust in me. Kasabian was never one for such formalities and protocol though, and he rushed over to me, embracing me in his muscled arms. My body froze. I didn't have the desire to hug him back; the only set of arms I wanted were Lux's. If only the wavy hair that brushed my face was longer and straight, if only the eyes that stared at me were sharper and darker. For a moment, I could picture it, the prince with raven hair and a seductive smirk. But the illusion gave way to reality, and my fingers dug into my palms.

"I'm sorry, Val," Kas murmured as he released me.

I sniffled, urging the water in my eyes to stay put as I looked up at the sky. "Debrief me on what happened while I was away."

Kasabian filled me in as we walked into the castle, leaving the stable boys to care for our mounts. Zasper and Dryden trailed behind us, Citadel having already left to meet with Commander Mordris and Head Guard Falchor who had adjusted well to their promotions after overthrowing Vukan.

"Well, nothing of particular importance happened while you were away. A few vassals to King Stallian came, seeking the traitor's freedom, well more so demanding it, perhaps trying to take advantage of their queen's absence."

I cocked a brow. "Oh?"

Kasabian grinned with a mischievous mirth . "Since they were so concerned about their King, I had them placed in adjoining cells to put them at ease."

My lips curled, a sweet satisfaction warming my face. "You know aiding in the kidnapping of the queen's consort deserves nothing but the best accommodations. Did you interrogate him?" I asked, my words tinged with cold ire.

"Since he already admitted to you on that day that he handed over His Highness to... What did you say his name was?"

"Noctis." The hair on my skin raised and all warmth vanished.

Kas snapped his fingers. "Right. Since he already admitted that, he couldn't deny it now. But he refused to divulge anything else about how he knew Noctis or where His Highness is being held."

I balled my hands into fists, vowing that the worms would feast on Dumas' body.

As our footsteps echoed in the halls and as we passed saluting guards, I whispered, "Any signs of the former Legate?"

He shook his head. "The last we saw of him he was crossing into Eboc, and King Mamba relayed to us that they kept eyes on him until he passed into Manchur. There has been no sign of him since."

"Manchur..." I mumbled. I wondered what he was doing there, if he was well. My heart ached at the thought because, despite our unfortunate end, I still wished for him to realize the errors of his ways and for him to live a good life.

Kasabian said there had been no word sent from any of the other kings concerning Noctis or Lux's whereabouts. King Mamba had also inquired when the Ebocian's second princess would be returning. I glanced at Zasper. It was her choice, but I was torn if I wanted her to return to her home or not. We hadn't talked much on the return trip, but no matter how frustrated I was with her, she was still my friend. I would have to discuss what she wanted to do at a later time.

First I needed to meet with Mordris and Falchor. As I walked to my office, I rubbed my temples. Stupid head.

The men waited, standing behind a table with a map of Racour splayed on top. I noticed for the first time how little color was left in Mordris' hair, and more lines had appeared on Falchor's forehead and around his eyes. A mixture of battles and time had accelerated their aging, but I was certain that Mordris would never retire, that he would keep his post until he returned to the ground.

"Your Majesty," they said in tandem, saluting with their fists to their palms.

I waved my hand, and they relaxed, letting their arms hang by their sides. "There weren't any attempted coups while I was away, right?" I asked with a chuckle.

Mordris placed both palms on the table, shaking his head. "No. I've been monitoring the people's sentiment via the generals in all the regions. It seems that as of right now, the citizens of Racour are grateful for Vukan's eradication."

"And within the palace and Pardus, everyone seems to be sympathetic towards Your Majesty," Falchor added. His voice dropped low, his lips downturned. "What do you plan to do next?" he asked, eyes boring into me.

I pinched the bridge of my nose. "I don't know. First, I need a moment alone to think about things. So if there is nothing else, I will depart for my quarters now."

The two men shook their heads, saluting as I left the office.

"Get some rest, Your Majesty!" Mordris hollered as I disappeared out the door.

I headed to my rooms as I was in desperate need of a proper bath. Everything was the way I had left it, the sofa, armchair and table by the fireplace, and the white canopied bed backed against the center of the wall. I stormed straight to the bathing room as servants scurried ahead of me and drew the water. I averted my eyes to the paintings Lux had created that were hanging around, evidence of him—screaming his absence. I stripped my clothes off and ordered the servants to leave, perhaps with too harsh a tone. I would apologize later, but I was was struggling to hold back the tears at this point.

The saddle sores on the inside of my thighs stung as I sunk myself in the warm water. I would need to apply an ointment and wrap them. As the water washed over my body, a feeling of guilt overwhelmed me. Shame seared into me like a cattle brand as I was sitting in a luxurious warm tub while Lux was suffering. Was he hungry? Was he hurt? Was he doubting my dedication? Did he think I wouldn't come for him? If I was Zasper, perhaps not.

Her pragmatic personality would make her an effective ruler one day. Her older sister, Shani, had already made it clear she had no intentions of ruling, making Zasper next in line to inherit the kingdom of Eboc. She would not doubt herself, would not be indecisive. She always made a choice and stuck to it, having no qualms about sacrificing a few for the good of the many. I was the complete opposite, and our differences in personality had been the source of contention over the past couple of weeks.

I submerged my head under the water. My poor attempt at drowning out my thoughts. Staying under until I was forced to surface, my lungs burned as I gasped, gulping down precious air. I got out of the water and dried myself, having instructed the servants to stay out until I said otherwise. I dressed in the clothes they left folded on a chair near the tub.

Slipping my arms through the drooping linen sleeves, I wrapped the top around my waist and knotted it off, and then I tied the pleated skirt around me, my fingers brushing against the wisteria flowers embroidered on the cloth. So beautiful, so delicately sewn, so luxurious compared to what most could afford. Hopefully one day I could develop Racour's economy and ensure the wealth was distributed so that all could afford such things. But that would have to wait because I needed my consort before I could focus on governing.

As soon as I entered the bedroom, a scaly body slammed into me. I stumbled, trying to catch my balance as Bahm wrapped himself around my torso, his cobalt head rubbing my chest.

Bahm's golden eyes beamed up at me, and although I had spent little time with them, it looked like he was asking, *Where is Lux?*

My hand gently caressed the scales of his neck. "I'm sorry. We couldn't find him."

A pitiful screeching sound came from the dragon, and I could have sworn the golden light of his eyes darkened. A hissing whistle brought my attention to Sol who was sitting on the floor with her tail wrapped around her legs like a big house cat. The emerald she-dragon looked angry, probably because I hadn't taken them with me on our expedition, concerned that keeping track of them would impede our efforts.

"I miss him too! I want him back too!" I yelled, my voice shrill and cracking like glass, my emotions fraying and still worn out from our failed trip. I couldn't hold back the tears anymore as I collapsed to the floor, and Bahm nuzzled my hair as I let out the sobs. I pounded my fist against my thigh as if the pain in my leg could distract me from my internal anguish.

Suddenly, the green dragon appeared in front of my face. Through blurred vision I watched her own violet eyes take in mine. Sol's tongue flicked in and out, and a slow long whistle sounded. I wasn't sure exactly what it meant, but Sol touched her snout to my nose. I took it as her attempt at comforting me, and I wrapped my arms around both the dragons, causing a small squeak to come out of Sol.

A scratching noise at the door ended our tender moment. I opened the door to find Dryden standing in waiting, but before he could say anything, a blue blur bolted, colliding with the big gray cat. Bahm had been infatuated with the ice leopard since they had first met, although Dryden only tolerated the small creature.

I couldn't help but laugh, wiping my nose as Dryden grumbled, *I'm going to kill it one day.*

I did my best to scold him through my giggling, *Don't you dare.*

Previously, Dryden and I were forced to keep apart for his safety, our magical bond creating an aching in our hearts when we were absent from each other. I was happy to have him with me now. However, I exchanged one ache for another as I yearned for Lux. I scratched Dryden's muzzle, and his expression calmed. Bahm continued to sit between the cat's enormous paws. Sol rested on the hearth—her favorite spot. She stared at Dryden, perhaps wary, ready to help her partner if there were any signs of aggression from the ice leopard. Animals had a way of comforting humans, and I was grateful for all of them during such a trying time.

Laughter chased away the tears, at least temporarily. I walked to my vanity and brushed out my hair. It was still wet from the bath, but I was too exhausted to dry it. Instead, I attempted to ball it atop my head and pin it, but a stray section continued to flop out. As my fingers fumbled and tried to twist it just right, I felt my nose start to sting again, my hands shaking.

Soft hands enveloped mine, and I jerked, my ribs slamming into the wooden table, barking in pain. I whipped around to see Rosalva—just as attentive as she was when she took care of me following Zenith's death and me getting whipped—smiling sympathetically, graying hair piled in a neat bun on her head. Her wrinkled face was a welcome sight as she wiped the hair from my face with a gentle touch. She smelled of roses and fresh linens.

Her raspy voice spoke as her eyes seemed to gaze deep into me, seeing the guilt that plagued me, "Don't worry, honey. It's not your fault."

I folded into her embrace, holding onto her words even tighter. They were words I desperately needed to hear, even if I couldn't believe them yet.

She patted my back as she whispered, "The Creator is watching over him, so don't worry too much."

I nodded, accidentally smearing snot onto her sleeve. I pulled away and wiped my face. "Sorry about that."

She waved her hand as if it were nothing. "It is my honor to serve my queen."

Rosalva's skilled and deft hands made quick work of my hair. She retied the sash binding my robes, creating a pretty bow shape with the long strips of cloth. I thanked her once again as I walked out of my room and into the hallway, Dryden and the dragons in accompaniment, while Rosalva stayed behind to tidy up the bathing room.

Falchor was waiting outside, his silver armor shining in the noon light. An ice leopard adorned with a crown atop its head had been painted over the embossed Wulfric wolf on his breast and shoulder plates. Painting the High Queen's sigil was a cheaper and quicker endeavor than commissioning new armor which would have only served my ego and not the commoners who had paid atrociously high taxes for nearly a decade under the Wulfrics.

Seeing as there were no other guards present, it must have been his turn to be on duty. Post the coup to end Vukan's reign, our military ranks were left in tatters, some from death and others retiring, and thus only one or two guards at a time were ever stationed by me. I was not concerned though. As long as it wasn't Noctis, I could handle myself.

Despite the sharp lines of his jaw and cheeks, his eyes were still soft, and as we made our way to the throne room, he asked, "Are you alright, Your Majesty?"

Was it that obvious that I was breaking? I nodded, unable to give a verbal answer. I hated that question. It was as sharp as a sword, able to crack the wall that held all of my emotions. If I answered aloud, the wall would crumble, and I couldn't allow that. I had to endure a while longer. Instead, I changed the subject. "How is your son?"

Falchor beamed, his posture straightening. "He started walking while you were away. He even started talking. My wife says it's just blubbering, but I swear I heard him call me 'Dad'."

"Sounds wonderful. I am sure he will grow to be just as capable as his father."

Falchor's chest puffed out ever so slightly.

Humans can be so strange, Dryden snickered.

I glanced at him. *What was strange about our conversation?*

Dryden's lips twitched. *Why would he be proud of his child? He puffed up like a peacock's plume when you complimented his son.*

Do ice leopards take no pride from their offspring? I asked incredulously.

Dryden's whiskers twitched as his head inclined. *We gain satisfaction from our own accomplishments. What our cubs do or don't do is not attributed to the sires. Of course, we are fiercely protective of them, but it tends to be the clan as a whole who raises them.*

As interested as I am in learning more about ice leopards, I teased, *I need to focus on the conversation you so rudely interrupted, so please hold off on the disparaging of us humans for the time being.*

The big cat bumped me with his shoulder, causing me to stumble.

Falchor caught my elbow. "My Queen! Is something wrong?"

I glared at Dryden. "No. I'm alright. I just lost my footing for a moment."

As we entered the throne room, I took in all who were present. Princess Zasper was in a wrapped skirt and top, King Kasabian who had changed into more luxurious robes, Legate Citadel still in his armor although with clean garments underneath, and a few nobles that I recognized as vassals to House Stallian.

I jutted my chin out, doing my best to present an air of regality instead of fatigue. I walked up the dais with a posture as straight as a pillar and turned, casting my robes aside as I sat on my throne, my hands running over the carved ends that resembled leopard paws.

I inhaled a deep breath before addressing the court. "What is it that you wish to discuss?"

The lord who stepped forward was Tavian Rubin with the pale skin of the northerners. I remembered their faces that so shamelessly stared at me that day they threw my husband away—remembered the look of fear in their eyes as ice exploded around them along with my fury.

He bowed, speaking as his blond hair dangled in front of his forehead, "Your Majesty, we have gathered to request the release of our King Stallian."

I raised a brow, my voice as low as a crouching ice leopard. "I remember you, Lord Rubin. You were with Dumas when he gave my husband away."

"Your Maj—"

"Do you remember, Lord Rubin, what I promised if I could not find my husband unharmed? If I returned here without him?" I channeled all my icy rage into my eyes, daring them to try me further. "I do believe that I promised to execute him on the grounds of treason. Are you pleading for the life of a traitor? Are you aligning yourself with such a person?"

Tavian gulped, sweat forming on his forehead as he looked at his comrades, unsure how to respond. "Of-of course not, Your Majesty. I simply—"

"Good." I paused to stand, flicking a nonexistent piece of dust from my shoulder. "I was afraid we would have to expand the prisons for fear that they would become too full."

I waved over the stewards Kasabian had ordained while I was away. Myra Silvus was a woman with dark brown hair graying at the roots, sun spots on her face, and a thin frame. She had been the wife of the previous steward under my mother, and apparently, she had been just as adept as her late husband, although her aptitude would have been dismissed under Vukan. Next to her was Thaddeus Romana, an older gentleman with glasses and a rather large bald spot and a short and chubby figure. Kasabian assured me he was very capable, having kept the books for many merchants in Gwanji.

They both came forward and bowed.

"I hereby decree that Dumas Stallian is deposed as the king of the northern region, and his territory will be given to another. Likewise, Labin Flock, Strallick Vernyn, Harmon Fernal, and Mervin Pomier will all be stripped of their lands and titles due to their collaboration with the traitor. Dumas Stallian will be executed tomorrow at dawn, and his lords exiled from the region. Their families may stay if they so choose."

Citadel stepped forward, his brows drawn together, hand resting on the end of his sword. "Your Majesty, I am concerned that their families could retaliate."

My hand rubbed against my collarbone as I contemplated. "I will not punish one for the sins of another. If they decide to do something foolish in the future, they shall be dealt with accordingly," I replied with finality.

He bowed, but I could see the protest lingering in his face, his grip tightening on his hilt. I prayed I would not regret my mercy.

Next, I addressed the stewards, who were in charge of many administrative duties. "I trust you to find suitable replacements for their positions. Bring me a list of names by tomorrow evening."

They bowed in tandem. "Yes, Your Majesty."

I looked back at Tavian and the remaining lords. "I expect you to serve your new king with loyalty and respect."

The men gave a stuttered response, "Yes, Your Majesty."

I waved them away, tone cold and hard. "Get out."

They rushed to exit, stumbling towards the doors.

Dryden laughed next to me. *That was entertaining. I could smell their fear.*

As soon as they all exited, my shoulders slumped, but I was relieved to know that I had properly intimidated them. I switched my attention to my friends, where Kasabian was holding in laughter while Zasper nodded in satisfaction.

My stomach growled, and I realized I hadn't eaten since returning. "Shall we go to the dining hall? I could do for a good meal."

We made our way to the dining room, discussing any other potential threats or issues that the House Stallian vassals could create. I doubted they would be able to start a rebellion, seeing as how, after House Galapos, Stallion had the lowest population as the harsh territory became more difficult to inhabit the further north one went.

The people's favor was with me for now. However, the love of the citizens could just as easily turn to dissatisfaction—the breeding ground for uprisings. For the time being, we all concurred that such an event was not probable, and our biggest threat was Noctis. Indo had been all too happy to receive the peace treaty I had sent after reclaiming the castle, and we were on good terms with the rest of Saego. News would have spread of my magic, my ice leopard, and the dragons, and since stories tended to become bigger than reality the more they were passed on, I felt confident that tales of giant scaled beasts and entire defense walls of ice were being whispered across the land.

After exhausting every possible problem, we arrived and took our seats. I'd told the head servant of the dining hall how many places to set, and now a person was sitting behind each dish except for one. There was an empty plate and a vacant chair next to me.

A servant scurried to my right, reaching out to remove the unused cutlery and dishes.

"Don't. Touch. It." I hissed, my grip tightening on my utensils.

The poor man slinked away, skin pale and eyes wide. Lux's place at the table would stay there until he came home.

Zasper stared at me unapprovingly, her lips pursed and head shaking in a slight motion that felt like severe scolding to me, but I ignored her and asked, "What am I supposed to do about Noctis? Our search proved fruitless, and there has been no helpful information sent to the palace." My voice was starting to break, my emotions causing it to shake like branches in a storm.

"Perhaps it is time to give up searching for him yourself and instead—"

I broke her off, my hand slamming into the table and rattling the dishes. "Don't finish that sentence."

Thankfully she didn't push it, her gaze peeling away from me and turning to her meal.

Kasabian's brow furrowed and his eyes narrowed for a moment before speaking. "Perhaps," he paused, rubbing the sprouting facial hair on his jaw, "there may be answers in another place."

"Where?" I demanded, my voice shrill and the question filled with the eagerness of a starving man being presented with food.

The former pirate lord looked up, eyes dancing. "Would you like to finally see the sunset with me, Val?"

He was talking about his homeland on the other side of Eboc, the land of deserts, oases, and some sort of creature called camels, the land we had made plans to see all those years ago. I glanced at Zasper, who was already shaking her head, words of disagreement poised on her lips.

I turned back to Kasabian and spoke before she could voice her opposition, "To Percia then."

CHAPTER THREE

VALINE

My *bags were packed* with just the essentials. It would be a long trip over a far distance, so I couldn't take too much with me. Despite the protest of my servants who insisted on helping me—to which I declined—I shoved a spare change of clothing into the bag along with a few tinctures of medicine and bandages just in case trouble found us, as it seemed rather infatuated with me.

Next to my pack was a crossbow with a quiver of bolts, along with a scroll bearing the image of Lux, the sharp pang of an arrow hitting my heart every time I saw it. I shoved the yearning away and the painting into a cylindrical container and adjusted its strap across my chest. I had suggested that my servants who were so intent on packing my things to instead handle the group's supplies: food, bedrolls, and weapons.

Our retinue included myself, Dryden, Sol and Bahm, Kasabian, and Citadel. Even though the Legate's duty was to maintain the palace soldiers, Citadel had originally been Lux's personal guard, as well as having protected me while I was a prisoner. Having him with me felt like having a little bit of Lux, so Falchor, despite being in charge of the queen's private guards, would remain here in his stead.

While we were away, Ravi and Raia—who had aided in my rebellion—would be in charge of Armani territory until its new king could return. They were also from Percia, just as Kasabian was, so, although they missed their home country, they wanted to take care of their new one. As for the dragons...well according to Kas, they had wreaked utter havoc when I was away, and all the staff refused to enter the room with them. Thus, for the sake of all in the palace, Sol and Bahm would accompany us.

Bahm dangled from Dryden's tail as the big cat's eyes threatened violence. Sol, content to bask in the sunlight pouring through the window, kept one eye pinned on Bahm in case Dryden decided to enact the thoughts in his head. So much for the protective rumors of big scary beasts roaming the courts of Pardus.

"Being your regent is just an excuse," Zasper hissed, her glaring eyes and frowning lips the epitome of her displeasure at being left behind to watch over the kingdom.

I didn't turn to face her, continuing to arrange my things. "You are a good leader. Right now that is very much needed in Racour."

"You should be the one leading it," she replied her voice barbed with condescension, each word digging into my already hurting heart. "Did you even choose replacements to appoint as new lords for the ones you're going to exile? You can't only delegate it to the stewards."

"First of all, I already handled that this morning. And are you suggesting I leave Lux to suffer whatever horrific fate is befalling him?" I asked, despite knowing how my pragmatic friend would answer.

"Send out your soldiers to look for him. Don't disregard your other responsibilities for the sake of one man," Zasper urged.

I spun around, nostrils flaring. "Would you leave me? If it was myself and not Lux, would you come for me?" I questioned, staring into her eyes.

Her silence was her answer.

I shook my head, my hand tightening around the strap of my pack. "I am not like you, Zasper, and I never intend to be." I shoved a spare dagger into my bag. I couldn't help the bitter jealousy that tinged my words. "You have your family. You always had a home. You have no idea what I have been through, what I have endured. I am not like you. I am not willing to throw people away for my own benefit, and I will not treat others as a means to an end." I slung my pack over my shoulder and brushed past my friend, pausing in the doorway and taking one last look at her.

She was so smart, so clever, her soft shape obscuring the sharp steel beneath. She was well-versed in making the hard choices that were an innate a part of ruling. A small seed of doubt sprouted.

Was I doing the right thing? Was Zasper more fit to be queen than someone so emotional as myself? Was my sentimentality a weakness?

No.

The Creator made me this way, made everyone with different personalities—different strengths and weaknesses—so that when we came together we could be each other's strengths. She could quell my impulsiveness while I could help her see different perspectives. A balance of emotion and logic, but that logical side had lost me Sokah. I didn't care if it wasn't the practical thing to do, if it was irresponsible as the ruler of Racour, I would not leave Lux to die.

My heart ached, as it so often did these days. "I would search the entire world until I found you, Zasper." I didn't wait for her to reply, couldn't bear to look at her face, at the sure judgment that would be painted there, and I left the room and made my way to the castle's entrance with animals in tow.

So many thoughts occupied my mind as I walked down halls and stairways. At the forefront of my mind was Lux. I lifted a prayer up. *Please let him be okay. If you could tell him I'm coming, tell him to hold on a little longer, I would appreciate it.*

Honestly, I wasn't sure if it worked that way, but that's what Egann had done. My deceased mentor often spoke about how The Creator spoke to him, and I was jealous, wishing He would be so clear with me too. I sighed as I reached the doorway that led outside. The guards opened them, revealing the members of my group waiting for me.

Citadel, his brown hair recently cut short, was saying farewell to Mordris and Falchor, the former going out into Racour searching for answers concerning the whereabouts of the queen's consort.

Meanwhile, Kasabian was speaking to himself, practicing some conversation only he was privy to as he was using his native tongue, a deep, throaty-sounding language that was difficult to learn as a Racourian since our language favored softer sounds and the front of our mouth. Dryden kept a careful eye on the dragons. Bahm ran between the ice leopard's legs while Sol sat aside, watching over her brother. Dryden's ears flattened, his nostrils flaring.

I hate the sand. And the heat. He paused to growl at Bahm as the cobalt dragon pounced on the leopard's tail once more. *And these infernal oversized lizards.*

Are you going to complain the whole trip? I asked, readjusting my grip on my packs and cracking my stiff neck.

Dryden whipped his tail away from Bahm, tufts of fur floating in the air from the jarred movement, but it only caused the dragon more amusement as he leaped, trying to catch the chunks of hair before they fell or floated away.

Can't we leave them here? he whined.

I strode towards him, setting my bags on the ground, and scratched his head, careful to avoid his ears. *You're lucky we're bonded, otherwise I'd be leaving you behind.*

He towered over my kneeled position as a pitiful whimper emitted from the big cat, *You don't mean that.*

A smile pulled at my lips, and I stood to meet his eyes. *You know I don't. For better or for worse, we are bound for life.*

He rubbed his head against my chin, his purrs louder than a thunderstorm.

I pulled away as the stable boys brought out our horses, who were shifting their long legs in nervousness—always uncomfortable around Dryden. I walked up to the gray gelding that I rode previously, grabbing his reins in one hand and scratching his muzzle with the other. He snorted and a warm breath blasted into my face.

I made my way to the saddle-bags draped over his back. A bedroll and rations had been prepared in one pack, so I put my things in the other. I hung my crossbow and quiver on the pommel of the saddle, my sword dangling in its sheath on the other side. Running my hand along his neck, I realized I never asked for his name before. I looked around for one of the stable boys. A young, pudgy boy with blond hair and big ears stood nearby.

"Hey, what's this one's name?" I called out.

The blond boy whipped around and stuttered, "Tempest, Yo-Your Majesty."

I crinkled my nose. "What kind of name is that?"

"Some soldiers named him that because he has such a bad temper around them," he replied. "He only ever let the court ladies ride him despite being a war horse."

"And it got him turned into a gelding," another stable boy with chestnut hair and freckles mumbled.

I leaned my head against Tempest's hide. Animals remembered, and if they had suffered abuse in the past, they would come to hate whoever resembled the source of their pain. It could be a man or woman, someone with certain colored hair, or even a type of clothing. I inhaled the scent of hay coming off of him. Poor Tempest. I wondered what terrible experience he'd had in the past, about what those soldiers had done to him.

The principles of a leader trickled down to their subordinates, and Vukan had not lacked cruelty. And what about me? What example was I? I gritted my teeth as a rock hard determination settled in my gut to protect those in my care.

I leaned back, looking into his brown eyes. "I won't let anyone hurt you."

Tempest whinnied in return, and I smiled, kissing the soft area between his nostrils.

"I miss the days when you kissed me," Kasabian's voice interrupted.

"It was one time, Kas, and that's inappropriate," I scolded. "Besides, I am your queen and a married woman now."

Kasabian bowed. "My apologies, Your Majesty." He stood upright, face turning serious as his jaw clenched. "We should be going though. Sun is almost up."

I nodded, and we all mounted our horses, exiting the palace walls and heading towards Pardus. The quickest way to Percia's capital city was to board a boat at the border village of Kenobi on the Eboc side, and from there we would sail on to Terran, the capital of the desert country.

The closer we got to the city center, the more crowded it became. Light crested over the horizon, signaling the start of a new day, but it was more than the usual early risers who had to start work in the morning. Something else was drawing out so many people at dawn.

The same platform that had been raised a little over a month ago was set up once more. The caged wagon surrounded by soldiers was also in the same place, but this time, only one occupant stood behind its bars. Dumas

Stallian lost weight during the month he had been incarcerated, and his expensive garments were dulled by the grime of the dungeons.

Compared to the previous executions of the clear traitors to my crown, the crowd was more subdued, and I could only assume they were unsure why one of the five kings was here. There had been many rumors, which only a few like myself knew were true, that Dumas had assisted Vukan and Gabrys Wulfric in their coup against my mother, but to the commoners, they were only unconfirmed whispers.

We brought our horses to a halt near the wooden stage, and I dismounted and climbed up the stairs, my feet slamming against the wood like a drum, Citadel following closely behind like a mother hen. I gazed out over the crowd. Some looked a little too excited for the execution, and my stomach twisted in revulsion. Seeing someone die was haunting, even if it was done in the name of justice.

I cleared my throat and began, "Today we have gathered to execute justice once again."

"You crazy bitch! I hope you never find your husband, you—"

A guard cut him off, slamming the pommel of his sword into Dumas's head. The disgraced king clutched his skull with his iron bound wrists, blood seeping between his fingers. I glared at him. He was making it easier for the words to come out of my mouth.

"Dumas Stallian assisted in the kidnapping of the Prince Consort, Lux Polaris. He refused to repent and assist the crown in search of the consort. Thus he has committed treason, and his sentence is death," I yelled over the crowd.

Dumas soiled himself as he was hauled next to the noose, the smell of urine permeating the air.

"Please," he blubbered, all fight having melted into desperation as the guard placed the rope around his neck. "I'm sorry. I really don't know where that freak took him. I—"

I didn't allow him the opportunity to finish, waving my hand to signal the executioner. The soldier pulled the lever, releasing the floor beneath the deposed king. Dumas's face turned red when the rope went taut, the fat around his neck kept the fall from breaking it. As he suffocated, saliva foamed in thick bubbles, resembling that of a rabid dog, as Dumas clawed at the rope. After a few minutes, the writhing ceased, and his hands fell to his side.

The crowd murmured, a few daring to cheer. Many were already scurrying off to go about their daily responsibilities. Were they indifferent to such things, to anything that didn't affect their lives as long as they had food on the table? I worried for a moment, that perhaps they had become too accustomed to death over the past several years, that they had simply grown used to seeing it. Vukan had publicly killed many during his bloody reign, and I didn't want to make it a habit of mine. I wished for my reign to be associated with peace and prosperity, but so far it was having a tumultuous start.

As I walked back down the steps and mounted Tempest, I hoped there would be no need for more executions. The soldiers helped clear a path, and we galloped out of the city, leaving its troubles behind. I prayed that I would be able to create a secure and prosperous kingdom in which death was only caused by old age and where there was a plethora of food and shelter for all.

That dream would have to wait.

CHAPTER FOUR

Lux

My *stomach growled. I* wasn't sure how much time had passed. Hours? Days? Months? Time was irrelevant in the darkness. I held onto the good memories, however few there were, to keep myself from descending into madness. I reminisced about my sweet mother—her amber eyes and raven hair, her soft, round face. I recalled the koi fish in the courtyard pond, a pool of crystal teal surrounded by lotus flowers and stalks of green bamboo that the wind would whistle through like a flute. We would feed them by hand, and their small mouths would suck at our fingers, creating a funny sensation. She would read stories to me at bedtime, giggling and smiling until I drifted off to sleep.

But then those blissful memories would shatter, revealing the image of her hanging by a rope next to my aunt.

Then I tried to move on to Valine, my Little Bird. I thought of her tenacity and compassion, of her love of sweet tarts, but then those too were manipulated into a terror that hadn't even occurred. Valine choked on the pastry, her face turning red then blue, her body contorting as she writhed and fought for air.

I banged my head against the metal bars, trying to banish such images from my mind.

Laughter echoed in the void of black. "The little pup looks so funny when he's scared." A hot, wet breath caressed my neck as the thing continued, "You are weak, just like your father."

"I am nothing like my father!" I spat.

"Oh no?" The creature sneered. "You are more alike than you wish to admit." The voice within my head sent a shudder down my spine. *You are so much like him, even your wives couldn't stand you both. Your mother hated you and your father so much she chose death.*

"No!" I yelled back. "She loved me!"

Then why did she kill herself? If not to end her suffering caused by you and your father?

The voice always tried to manipulate me, his cleverly crafted lies based on the truth, and it was getting increasingly more difficult to distinguish the two. Lies repeated over and over resembled reality more and more.

I turned to the one thing that silenced it. *Creator, please help me. I don't know how much longer I can take it.*

The creature's voice disappeared from my head, and it hissed, retreating away from my cell like one would from a hot flame.

If only the fire that had once been so easy to beckon were to appear again, to burn away the darkness and melt my prison bars, but there was something strong suppressing my magic. No matter how badly I willed it, the flames never came, reduced to nothing more than a smoldering ember beneath my skin. My fingers had wandered every inch of the cage and found strange etchings in the metal, but there was nothing else to see or feel. The only sounds were occasional scuttering of what I assumed were rats, water dripping, and of course the grating voice of the creature. The smell of death permeated the air, but at this point, my nostrils had grown accustomed to the putrid stench. I grew nauseous every time I thought about what was creating the smell.

My thoughts wandered to Raven Bone, the blind shadow wielding chief of the Waodani. Perpetual darkness was all he had ever known, yet such a disability—deemed pitiable by Racourians—was revered by the Waodani. Those who were born blind were considered full of wisdom, their lack of sight forcing them to self-reflect more, develop skills and senses that made them unique. And although the attributes and history of magic was not well known in the Waodani people, those born blind were always gifted with shadow magic.

Or perhaps it was the other way around and once one was chosen as chief their sight was taken. Maybe The Creator took one thing in order to give another, using ailments or deformities to keep his creatures humble. Or maybe none of it was true, all convoluted rumors and assumptions about the mysterious people. Valine and myself had no such ailments, although I had headaches since childhood, but we certainly had our fair share of other hardships.

I sighed, a desperate yearning for my wife digging into my heart. I had given her the nickname, Little Bird, since she was captured and brought to the castle because she resembled a majestic bird confined to a cage. I laughed to myself.

How ironic.

Now I was the one trapped in iron bars.

It gave me a newfound sympathy for how hard that time was for Valine. She was so precious, and her heart, unlike her magic, remained tender and warm. She had given up her revenge for forgiveness and justice, unlocking a cage of her own making. She had helped me escape my own hatred as well.

Oh Valine...

At first, I never doubted she would come for me, but now, I was not so sure.

The creature's words echoed. *She hates you.*

I crushed the seeds of doubt that it had planted, refusing to allow those lies to sprout. She was coming for me. She was fiercely loyal and stubborn. She would come.

She had to.

CHAPTER FIVE

Valine

Our horses were exhausted. In our urgency, we rode the entire day, only stopping for short breaks to drink and eat. By the time we arrived in the Sosoni village of Perce, our horses' coats were sweat covered, and white foam had formed on their hides. Dryden panted beside me, drained from keeping pace. Tempest's legs shook from the strain while his flanks heaved up and down.

"I'm sorry," I whispered as I slipped down from the saddle. "I know I promised to take it easier this trip, but I... I couldn't help myself."

"Just to be clear, we are resting for the night, right?" Kasabian asked, stumbling from his saddle-stiff legs; he was far more used to riding ships than horses.

I nodded, too tired to say more, all of us exhausted, except for Sol and Bahm, who had traded between gliding in the sky and riding on the rears of the horses. At one point, Bahm even tried to run next to Dryden, but gave up after falling behind.

The cobalt dragon was now mimicking Dryden, who was licking his sore paws. However, the scaled creature's slim tongue was unable to properly imitate the big cat's.

After taking a moment to stretch our limbs, we walked into the small village—one of the few permanent dwellings within Sosoni territory. We passed through rows of nomadic tents that made grazing their livestock easier. King Koodsin's estate of Triba was the only major city in the region, with a few villages along major routes like the one we were in.

Thankfully, it wasn't so small that it couldn't accommodate our group as well as the animals. This village often saw people traveling through it on to other houses of Racour or across the border, so despite the quaintness of the rest of the place, the inn was quite opulent with carved images of horses—the insignia of House Sosoni—on each of the top steps while the roof was layered with teal shingles that tapered into points at the corners after the fashion of Pardus. Whoever owned it must have had deep pockets. The rest of the town favored the simple triangular shapes of the rest of Sosoni structures, with beige and browns and the occasional grays blending in with the surrounding grasslands.

A servant boy ran out of the red-painted wooden doors to greet us and called out for another. A second boy emerged from the stables behind the building, straw protruding from his black hair. He shrieked at the sight of Dryden and the dragons, startling the birds nestled on the roof. Careful to steer clear of the ice leopard and dragons, the two wide-eyed and gaping boys grabbed the reins and led our horses to the stables.

As we trudged up the stone steps, my thoughts went to Tempest. I had promised that no one would mistreat him, yet I pushed him dangerously hard, had pushed us all too hard, in my urgency to get to Percia. Out of the corner of my eye, I saw Dryden limping.

I winced. *Are you alright?*

Dryden bared his teeth ever so slightly. *Ice leopards aren't made for long distance running.*

Tomorrow we will set an easier pace. Since we are in the village, I can even obtain a horse and cart to carry you.

I would never deign to be carried like that, he hissed.

I chuckled. Even when he was in pain, he was still too proud and stubborn.

The innkeeper—who was sweating more from the presence of the queen and the leopard insignia armor that Citadel wore—assigned us our rooms as I placed a pouch of coins on the counter and looked around the lobby. Fellow sojourners and locals alike drank to their heart's content, using the inn more like a tavern.

The inn was simple yet clean, with tasteful decor around the room. The ornate rug in the center of the floor was particularly beautiful, shades of yellow, orange, and red creating the image of a sunset. For most of my life, I either lived in or around Pardus. And while I did spend a year in Wulfric territory, I hadn't visited the other kings' domains. Seeing the unique designs of the decor made me want to explore more. After Lux and I were reunited, we could tour the country. He would enjoy seeing the different cultures, as I was certain his father had never been one for family travels.

Even within one country, there was no single culture, always slight variations and curiosities in every city and region. Architecture, accents, colloquial phrases, and foods all changed depending on the location. Red bean buns were a staple of Wulfric land, although I was curious how it would change under Kasabian's direction, while Galapos—to the surprise of no one—had the most decadent seafood. Stallian was infamous for their variety of potato dishes, and Sosoni was popular for goat milk and skewers. Roh produced the juiciest tangerines, although my favorite dish of theirs was spicy rice cakes. Thinking about it made my mouth water.

I paid the innkeeper extra to bring dinner to our rooms since we were all too exhausted to fight through the boisterous crowd in the dining area. Besides, it was the least I could do after pushing them so hard. The humped-back man didn't hesitate when I requested raw meat for Dryden and the dragons, filling his hand with even more coin. Despite seeing the creatures for the first time, he wasn't startled by their appearance, perhaps having seen many oddities in his line of business.

My hand ran along the wooden banister up to the rooms. The intricate carvings were something I'd never seen before and I imagined how much more Percia would differ from here as I had only traveled to one other country in Saego. When I was on the trading vessel all those years ago, we had only gone to Manchur—a country full of nomadic people famous for their riding skills and falconry. I caught a glimpse of the port city, but even in that short time I was amazed by the different clothing and food. Kasabian had talked one of the crew into obtaining some milk wine that the Manchurians had perfected over centuries. I loved it, but Kasabian had struggled to down the strong alcohol. Now I was finally traveling to see the Percian sunsets with him like we had talked about all those years ago.

I wished it was different circumstances that allowed me to do so.

As we headed up the creaking stairs, I handed out the keys the innkeeper gave me. "Kasabian, you and your ego are in one room, Citadel with the dragons, and Dryden, you're with me." If the dragons stayed with us, Dryden was sure to lose his temper.

"Your Majesty, please allow me to at least stand guard outside your rooms," Citadel argued, his brows drawn together and his lips pursed.

"You need to rest, Citadel. I know you're tired too, even if you try to hide it. Plus, I have a leopard with me. And if somehow that isn't enough for any would-be attackers, I can always freeze them."

The Legate considered it for a moment before agreeing, "As you wish, Your Majesty."

I closed the door behind Dryden and me, scanning the quarters and taking note of anything that could be used as a weapon—for or against me. There were no windows, as my room was in the middle of the hall, and the only pieces of furniture were a dresser on which a bowl and vase of water sat, a mirror, and a small desk and chair. It appeared that the majority of the inn's budget went to the exterior of the building and the main lobby. The bed centered in the middle against the back wall took up the majority of the space, and the sight of it reignited my exhaustion. I moved forward, letting my bags smack onto the floor and collapsed onto the bed. Dryden hopped up next to me, the furniture creaking from his weight.

You smell horrible. His nostrils flared.

I tried to shove him off the mattress, but he was too heavy. "You don't exactly smell like roses either."

Dryden licked at his paws. *I smell like I am supposed to.*

If you tell me I stink again, I will push you into the next body of water we come across, I threatened.

Dryden huffed but didn't reply.

Perhaps the fatigue caused the dam that held back my emotions to crumble because a wet tear fell from the corner of my eyes.

"Dryden, what if we can't find him?" I voiced my doubts at last.

Dryden shifted, laying his head on my stomach. *We will find him.*

"But what if we don't?" I pressed.

I won't let that happen. I respect your mate. He is a good fighter and a good man... I don't care if we search until we die.

I ran my hand through his fur, savoring its softness. "Why are you so determined to find him though?"

Dryden's ears flicked. *I may not be human, but ice leopards hold the mate bond as sacred. We mate for life, and even if our mate dies, we do not find another.*

Another tear dropped, my chest tightening in an all too familiar sensation. "I can't keep losing people, Dryden. My heart can't handle it."

I know.

Death was equality of life. No matter the power, wealth, or status one held, there was no outrunning death, no antidote, no avoidance of the inevitable invitation to the next life.

I knew Dryden wanted to promise that such a thing wouldn't happen. Despite his arrogance, he, too, had to admit that he was unable to control death, unable to overpower the forces of life that remained unseen. He was ferocious and loyal, but he could not protect everyone.

And neither could I.

My body was stiff and sore from riding the previous day as I rotated my neck and stretched out my legs. Dryden was splayed out on the bed, belly up and tongue hanging out. His breath reeked. I shoved him a little too hard, and the big cat fell off the bed with a thud.

He flipped onto his paws and snarled, *Was that really necessary?*

I tried to offer an apology, but I couldn't stop laughing at the sight of his hackles raised and claws unsheathed, far too similar to a house cat.

He stalked towards the door and attempted to open it, but his paw swatted uselessly against the handle. I opened it for him, a smile still plastered to my face. I knew he was upset, his pride hurt, but whether I was finally breaking under the pressure or tired from our ride, I continued to laugh. Dryden growled at me as he left the room.

Eventually, I calmed myself and grabbed my packs from the floor before heading downstairs, making sure to knock on Kas's door as I passed by, knowing that he was always the last to rise.

Citadel was already waiting, Bahm still asleep in his arms while Sol sat at his feet, although not due to any affection for the Legate. As soon as Dryden grew close, the cobalt dragon sprung to life and bolted towards the cat. Bahm flung himself under the leopard's stomach and rubbed against his furry legs. Laughter once again threatened to spill out, but I contained it with what little self-control I had.

The stairs creaked behind us, and I turned to see Kasabian rushing down, a pack slung over his shoulders.

We ate a hasty breakfast of eggs, rice, and vegetable pancakes before heading towards the stables. After giving the stable boys a little extra money, eliciting smiles and wide eyes, they stuttered their thanks and rushed off. We mounted our horses and set off in an easy canter.

I looked down at Tempest, his coat shining. The stable boys had given all the horses a good brush down. I ran a lock of his hair through my fingers. It was coarse and dry, but the color reminded me of Lux's own thick raven hair.

For a moment, the dark-gray mane became long, smooth, obsidian tresses.

I shook my head.

If I wanted to run my fingers through Lux's hair again, I needed to find him first.

The lock fell back against the dappled coat.

I looked towards the south-west. We were still a week and a half away from Kenobi, and from there it was another two days of sailing to Terran. I tightened my grips on the reins, frustrated with the pace we were forced to set. Dryden struggled to keep pace with the horses, but even if it damaged his dignity, we would have to obtain a wagon for the leopard to ride in. The only other option was to slow down even further, and I was unwilling to do so.

I glanced down at Dryden, who was already panting, pink tongue peaking through white fangs.

I hope you don't get wagon-sick.

You better not mean what I think you do, the ice leopard hissed.

Would you prefer to be sent back to Pardus? I asked, even though it was an empty threat.

Dryden snarled, *You couldn't make me if you tried.*

Then the wagon it is, I stated.

Dryden growled, but he didn't oppose it again. Though I felt bad for his wounded pride, I was more concerned for his condition. It was getting progressively hotter as we traveled south, and ice leopards were not built for such heat. We would have to make more frequent stops to rest and hydrate. Another delay. Another time consuming necessity that kept me from Lux.

In the next town, we bought a small, but sturdy, wagon and a young stallion to pull it. As a queen, I had significantly more money at my disposal than when I was a rebel princess—at least that was something to be grateful for, but I also knew I had to use it with great care. It wasn't *my* money to use frivolously, rather it was the blood and sweat of all of Racour.

Dryden sat upright in the wooden wagon, Sol on one side and Bahm on the other. As Bahm poked the leopard in his side, I knew I was going to hear many complaints for the rest of the trip.

Just don't eat him, I warned.

You didn't say I couldn't shove him off.

Be nice. He likes you so much. You should feel honored, I replied.

Dryden shifted, attempting to move away from the blue dragon, but Bahm simply followed.

I held in my laugh and brought Tempest into a canter.

We continued to travel as quickly as possible without endangering the health of our mounts. Tempest enjoyed being in front, biting at any horse who tried to overtake his position. Citadel followed close behind, eyes scanning for any danger or ambushes. I doubted that anyone would try. By now, word of my magic would have spread through all of Saego. Of course, there were other magic wielders somewhere out there, but I also had an ice leopard at my side, which no one else had. I was confident that no one would bother us.

Except for Noctis.

Whatever he was, he was powerful and elusive, and his magic seemed strange, nothing like I had seen. Egann had mentioned something or someone stealing magic. Perhaps he had been referring to Noctis. Or maybe Noctis was the vessel to some stronger, darker force. I prayed that we would be able to find the answers in Percia's extensive libraries.

Percia was the oldest country in Saego, having outlasted the rise and fall of many other kingdoms. Obsessed with history and record keeping, they maintained a lengthy roster of scribes and tome-keepers to ensure that their texts would never be lost. They were also the origin of the first prophet, a man named Abaram, who at the time likely seemed to be a lunatic, but he was the founder of the religion that followed The Creator—the state religion of Percia. Although Racour had no standard religion, many followed the ways of Abaram, such as I. Eboc also worshiped The Creator, the belief endorsed by Zasper's parents and generations of rulers before them. Manchur believed in no deity, simply in ghosts and spirits of nature. Indo, if I recalled correctly, believed in a multitude of deities, having thousands of temples across their country dedicated to each one.

I, however, thought the ways of The Creator were true. Even when I doubted if He was listening, I knew He was still there. I had ignored Him for a while, but not anymore. I needed His help now more than ever to find Lux.

Thus in our pursuit for answers and while clinging onto the remnants of hope I had left, we trudged on, the next three days blending together. Our routine was the same: ride, rest, ride, rest. Every night I'd offer a prayer, a plea for guidance and also some mercy. As if the situation weren't dire enough, the sores I'd developed from our last excursion were exacerbated from being on a saddle for such an extensive amount of time. I had never ridden a horse this long, and I was feeling the effects of it, constantly shifting my position in an attempt to relieve my skin. Only Citadel, who had ridden horses often as a soldier, was fine. The rest of us waddled whenever we dismounted, and I had to have Dryden look at a blister on my buttocks.

As Dryden and I made our way to the privacy of some green bushes, Kas ran up beside me.

"Want me to take a look at it for you?" he offered with a cheeky grin, eyes sparkling with mischief.

I punched his arm, leaving him to clutch the sore limb as Dryden sniggered, whiskers shaking. We found a thick patch of brambles to obscure us from the view of others. I was going to need to apply ointment and wrap them in some cloth to keep them from rubbing and getting worse. The ship suddenly didn't hold the same dread as it did before, offering a welcome reprieve from the saddle.

Before returning to the clearing where the others were waiting, I punched a birch tree, my skin breaking along with my patience.

We still had a day and a half until we reached Kenobi, and the closer we got the greater my eagerness became. It was the height of summer and the cicadas mocked us as we sweated and toiled on towards the border.

CHAPTER SIX
VALINE

The border between Eboc and Racour was not heavily guarded.

"You would think there would be more soldiers stationed here," Kasabian said, gesturing to the emptiness around us as we entered Eboc.

"Racour and Eboc have always been close allies," I explained. "Even under Vukan's reign, Eboc never sent more troops to fortify the border, likely in fear that such a military movement would be deemed a threat. King Mamba is known for his pacific tendencies, although I can't say the same for his daughters."

"Zasper sure can kill someone with one glare," he mumbled.

"Careful how you talk about her," I warned, my hands tightening on the reins.

"Alright, my bad. Sorry," he said, lifting his hands in surrender before grabbing a hold of his own reins.

From the border it was only one day's ride to Kenobi.

I pulled back on the reins until Tempest came to a stop. Turning in my seat, my sores stinging, I asked the group, "Should we stop, or can we ride through the night?"

I scanned their faces along with the horses. We were all dripping in sweat from the heat, but there was no white foam to be found on the horses' flanks or mouths, and their legs were steady as oaks.

"As long as we maintain an easy speed, I think we will be fine to keep going," Citadel answered, and Kasabian nodded in agreement.

I leaned to the side, patting Tempest's neck, his coat silky smooth from perspiration. "How do you feel, boy?"

The storm colored gelding shook his head with a snort, and I interpreted it as his approval.

We set a slow pace for the animals, but it would still bring us to the port city quicker than if we slept for the evening. We would get all the rest we needed on the ship. I prayed I would be able to sleep through the entire voyage. My sea-sickness was brutal and debilitating, and that one year on the trading vessel with Kas was more than enough sea-bound time for me.

We came to Kenobi, passing through the poorer wood thatched huts on the outskirts, and eventually the shanties gave way to the cubical buildings favored by the Ebocians. Squares and rectangles of varying red and brown hues were crammed in the port city, alleys snaking between buildings and colorful canopies covering the roads.

"I'll go to secure us a ship," Citadel said.

"I can go. *I* was a pirate after all," Kas quipped, puffing out his chest.

"Do you speak Ebocian?" Citadel raised a brow.

Kas's chest deflated, and I suppressed a laugh.

"Thought so," Citadel retorted, veering off from the group.

We led our horses to a stable while we waited. They were in need of a good brush and fattening oats. We paid the stable hands to take care of our mounts, and they accepted the Racourian coin, as most port cities had currency exchanges due to the international traffic.

One of the men shouted something in Ebocian at the sight of the ice leopard and dragons, his eyes wide as the full moon and his knees bent, ready to run. I ordered Dryden and the dragons to stay back at the sight of the quivering men. After our horses were handed over to the stable workers, we sat against a nearby tree, snacking on jerky and dried fruit, and I gave some jerky to the dragons and Dryden. The huge leopard looked hilarious, jaws smacking as he ate the dried meat.

Sol gulped hers down, while Bahm threw the jerky into the air before catching it in his mouth again and again. After Sol finished eating, she whistled, a quick and high pitched sound. Bahm immediately stopped playing with his food and slurped it down, and I couldn't help but chuckle.

I turned to the sound of approaching footsteps. Citadel strode towards us, a man, who I assumed was a sailor, close behind. The ebony-skinned man was bald and lean with loose flowing red clothes, and when he smiled he revealed an endearing gap in his front teeth.

The Ebocian man spoke, his words smooth and leaping like a dance.

"He said we can board right away Their merchant vessel leaves in one hour, and we will arrive in Terran in a day and a half. The season's currents are favorable for the trip, cutting off half a day," Citadel translated.

I stood, brushing the dirt from my pants. "Let's arrange board for the horses and then go to the ship. I'm sure we won't be gone for more than a couple weeks." I weighed the coin purse in my hand. The initial payment only covered one day, so we would need to go back to the stable to pay for the rest.

Citadel interpreted my command to the sailor. The man nodded, then replied in his native tongue, his gaze never leaving Dryden and the dragons. "He said he will wait for us at the docks," Citadel explained as the man scurried off, his head turning to stare at our animal companions until he disappeared around a corner.

Stares and whispers accompanied us, eyes drawn to the legendary dragons and ice leopard. Bahm relished the attention, holding his head high as he pranced through the streets, occasionally leaping from Citadel's shoulders to glide. Dryden on the other hand, walked protectively behind the blue dragon, and my lips tugged upwards. Sol perched on Kas's shoulder. She had taken a liking to him, which was rare for her.

Kasabian hummed as we walked, his heels bouncing as we got closer to the ocean.

"What song is that?" I asked, perplexed by the tune.

"It's an old Percian ballad," he said, offering no further explanation.

"How does it feel having left as a commoner and returning as a king of Racour?" I inquired, imagining how strange it would be to return to my home country as a leader of another nation.

"I have to admit, the steady pay that the position comes with is a lot nicer than looting. As far as going home, my mother will be ecstatic to see me, if we have time to visit her that is. I am the first born—her precious baby boy." He smiled and winked. "But my father..." his voice trailed off.

I cocked a brow, curious but unwilling to push the matter if he was reluctant to divulge more.

After a few moments, he replied with a sigh, "My father loves his nation very much, his family even more. I brought great shame to both when I left, and the fact that I am a king in a foreign land... Well, "I'm proud of you, son" is not likely to be what he says to me."

My shoulders hunched as my eyes turned to the sandy path we walked. "I'm sorry. That sounds hard," I muttered.

Kas shrugged. "It's fine. I gave up on receiving his approval a long time ago." He picked up his song again, and I took it that he wanted to end the conversation.

In contrast with Kasabian, his father sounded serious, and it was hard to imagine how such an obnoxious man could come from such a strict one.

The docks were bustling with men carrying heavy loads on and off the ships. Shouts rang out, ordering ropes to be untied or for sails to be hoisted. The salty smell of the ocean made me reminisce about the months I spent with Kasabian in Gwanji and on the ocean.

"Oh, my faithful lady!" Kasabian bellowed, arms spread out. His nostrils flared as he sniffed the air.

I chuckled and shoved him forward, Kas narrowly avoiding falling into the water.

He glared at me.

I shrugged. "What? I just wanted to reunite you with your lover."

Kasabian's outrage was short lived as we arrived at the ship that would take us to Terran. He ran his hand over the wood railing.

"Gorgeous," he whispered in appreciation.

The crew paused their preparations, faces filled with fear and awe as they took notice of Dryden, Sol, and Bahm. One man screamed and shimmied up the mast while another ascended the ropes hanging from the sails. Dryden stood a little taller, lips curling to reveal his canines, relishing the fearful respect they had for him.

A man, who I presumed to be the captain due to his extravagant hat filled with colorful feathers, approached us and gave a bow. Was it common for all captains to be this ostentatious? Kasabian would either get along with him, seeing as how similar they were in presentation, or he would resent the man for detracting from himself. It would be amusing seeing which it would be.

The man spoke with near perfect Racourian, likely a necessity of his occupation.

"Welcome aboard my humble vessel, Your Royal Majesty. I pray your trip will be comfortable and successful."

I glanced to Citadel, wondering what reason he gave for our travels. I could not read the blank face of the Legate, so I gave up, turning back to the feather-capped man.

"Thank you for allowing us to join your voyage on such short notice. How shall I address the captain of this fine vessel?" I inquired.

Dryden laughed. *Really playing it up for him, aren't you? Humans are so pretentious and insincere.*

I did my best to block him out and listen to the captain's response.

"You may call me Captain Baboa, Your Majesty," the man said as he took off his hat and placed it against his muscled chest.

I nodded in acknowledgement before speaking, "Forgive my impertinence, Captain Baboa, but our purpose is time sensitive. Is it possible to set sail immediately?"

Captain Baboa placed his hat back on his head, lips turned in a pleasant crescent. "Of course!"

He shouted in Ebocian to his crew, and suddenly everyone was rushing. Some untied the ropes holding the ship to the docks while others unfurled the sails. The bald man who had come to us with Citadel showed us to our room below the deck. As soon as the ship moved, I began to feel queasy. Somehow the fresh and salty smell of the ocean that made me feel relaxed and calm managed to turn into the worst stench imaginable once I stepped foot onto a boat.

It was going to be a long day and a half.

At the behest of the others, I got up and went onto the deck, hoping the sunshine and seeing my surroundings would help my seasickness. As my feet shuffled along the wood, I clutched my stomach, hunched over and afraid that any sudden movements would cause me to start retching again. The crew were rather relaxed compared to when we boarded since the breeze was strong enough to move us along but not so chaotic that there was much to do aside from minor adjustments.

On the far side of the ship, Kasabian was surrounded by a handful of the crew. They bellowed with laughter at whatever story he was regaling. I rolled my eyes but kept moving my feet. A rather robust wave rocked the boat, and I braced myself against the mast, my other hand covering my mouth. I hated this. I forced myself to inhale and exhale slowly, doing my best to focus on why I was on this damn boat. I was here for Lux. It would be well worth the hours of vomiting and fitful sleep.

A hand brushed my elbow, and I peered up from the deck to see Kasabian, concern etching his features.

"When your head is under water, it doesn't matter if it's a foot under or a hundred."

My head was aching too much for his riddles.

"What are you talking about?" I asked through gritted teeth, afraid that if I opened my mouth too wide, my stomach would take it as an invitation to vomit.

His brown eyes tinged with honey bore into me as he said, "I know you're struggling, and life has certainly been unkind to you. But you're not alone, Val. If you're drowning, call out for help. There are arms waiting for you." He gestured to where Citadel sat on a bench, eating dried fish, before he placed his hand over his heart. "I'm here for you."

I bit my tongue to keep the words from coming out. *You're not the arms I want.* Perhaps it was irrational, but I was afraid of others perceiving my relationship with the pirate-turned-king as anything other than friendship. In addition, I was angry at life for taking away the man I loved, the one I wanted, always leaving me behind in the wake of whatever disaster it wrought upon me.

"I'll be below deck if you need me," I said as I turned and shuffled back to the companionway.

Exhaustion finally overcame the nausea and allowed me to sleep. However, only nightmares welcomed me in my slumber.

Dark dungeons. Torture. Death.

I should have been an artist with how wonderful my imagination was. My mother would have been proud, if not worried, about how well I could conjure horrifying scenes.

After two attempts at sleeping, I gave up and stared at the wall, wishing that, for once in my life, something would come easy.

"You could at the very least help us find something useful in Percia," I said in a tone too harsh for addressing The Creator, but I was too tired, too frustrated to care or be sorry.

At least the winds were in our favor. I could be thankful for that.

CHAPTER SEVEN

VALINE

After a full day of vomiting—the sour taste still stuck in my mouth—I was grateful to hear that we were pulling into Terran's port. Clutching my stomach, I waddled my way to the deck to see the city. It was breathtaking. The capital of Percia was beautiful in a different way from Pardus and not just because Terran was located on the beach with palm trees intermingling with the buildings. The architecture was unique with the smooth, rounded domes on the palace and the flat tops of smaller buildings—similar to the Ebocian style—in contrast to Racourian sloped roofs. The structures were predominately all varying shades of beige, but there were splashes of colors from the red canopies and turquoise spheres on some of the larger buildings. I couldn't comprehend how they had gotten the rounded tops, how they didn't collapse.

As we docked at the port, I found myself unable to move, my eyes glued to the city.

Kasabian came up beside me. "Gorgeous, right?"

I nodded, mouth agape. "Yes."

Kasabian flung his hair over his shoulder. "The city is pretty too."

I elbowed him, and he laughed, the sound mixing with the crashing waves.

Our entourage made our way down the ramp and barnacle dotted dock and to the sandy shoreline. I bent down and grabbed a handful of sand, letting it run through my fingers. It was soft, almost silky, unlike the more coarse and rocky beaches that lined most of Racour. Sol's gaze never left Bahm as he jumped headfirst into the beach, disappearing under the yellow sand. The only indication of his location was the rippling lines as he slithered beneath the surface.

Bahm popped out of the sand, spraying Dryden in the face and eliciting a snarl from the ice leopard. I giggled at Dryden as his ears flattened in irritation.

Citadel cursed, shaking sand from his boots. "I will be cleaning sand out of everything for weeks."

Kasabian didn't mind, his nostrils flaring as he inhaled, a grin wide on his face. I flinched, my eyes instinctively closing as Kasabian made a loud cry with his tongue.

"What was that?" I questioned, shoving a finger into my ear.

"It's something we do in Percia when we are excited," he said smiling, his eyes as radiant as the sun above us.

We said goodbye to Captain Baboa and the crew and set off towards the palace.

As we approached, I was overwhelmed with the sheer massiveness of it. The walls were almost twice as high as those of my own castle, the parapet wide enough for three men to walk shoulder to shoulder. Percia's ancient palace was well maintained, as there was not a single crack to be found. Guards with spears lined the entrance, wearing tunics and sandals that had straps winding up their calves. They stared at the ice leopard and dragons through narrowed eyes. In tandem, they jutted their spears out to block the entrance.

Dryden growled, and the dragons hissed. I stroked the raised fur on the back of his neck.

Knock it off, I commanded Dryden, and he listened, his snarls ceasing. The dragons followed his lead, their hisses waning.

A guard with muscles large enough to crush a watermelon spoke in a gruff voice, and I waited, my eyes darting between him and Kasabian as they conversed. After a few more words were exchanged, the guards jerked their weapons back to their sides, their heads bowed as they gestured for us to enter.

"What did you say?" I asked as we strode through the sandstone entrance.

Kas glanced at me from the corner of his eye and shrugged. "I just explained why we came and that you were the Queen of Racour."

"And they just believed you because you're Percian?" Citadel asked, his tone tinged with disbelief.

"I'm a very convincing person," Kas replied with a chuckle and shrug.

Peeking out from under the top of the wide entry arch was a large metal gate that seemed to be controlled by some sort of pulley system. It was different from Racour's where we still used thick wooden gates that functioned like doors. Fountains and strange plants filled the courtyard like an oasis, a spot of green fighting to keep its place in the harsh desert country.

I could see where Kas got the appreciation of luxury, but my lip curled as I recalled the simple dwellings I had spotted on our way into the port. It seemed like an unnecessary waste of resources, a shallow beauty that did nothing to benefit the common folk.

The courtyard led into a covered area filled with hundreds of pillars and more fountains. How big was this place? My feet were beginning to ache, and my head was hurting from being out in the scalding sun. After what felt likes hours, we reached the palace doors, bringing an end to the palms and ponds, and we entered a high ceilinged room. There were murals of divine creatures painted on the walls and the floor was covered in tiles, creating a beautiful mosaic of reds, blues, and yellows.

I was about to ask Kasabian where to go when a woman appeared. She had tanned bronze skin and dark brown hair braided down the side. Her golden bangles and piles of necklaces jangled as she strode towards us, the orange silks she wore whispering as she walked.

Kasabian's eyes widened for a fraction of a moment. Before I could decipher if it was fear or shock or some other emotion, he masked it with a smirk.

With arms stretched out, Kas spoke with a smooth voice, "It's been—"

She came to a stop before Kasabian and slapped him across the face, the sound like crackling fire.

The pirate rubbed the red spot on his cheek. "Nice to see you too, Princess Naghmeh."

I gawked. Did the Percians have some sort of strange greeting custom I wasn't aware of?

Princess Naghmeh surveyed us, and my eyes widened and my mouth gaped as she spoke in Racourian, her gold jewelry jingling as she pointed at Kasabian, "How dare you show up after all these years. You ran away from our engagement, and now you show up with another woman?"

She spat at him, but he was more prepared this time and sidestepped the saliva. I looked at Kasabian, cocking a brow. Engagement? Was that the reason he had run away to Racour several years ago? Kasabian gave me a look, promising to explain later.

He turned his attention back to the furious princess, hands out in placation. "Princess Naghmeh, please, no one could compare to you."

The princess tossed her long brown braid over her shoulder, looking a little appeased as her chin and lips tilted up.

Kasabian continued, "I am simply accompanying the High Queen of Racour, Her Majesty, Valine Polaris." He bowed and gestured towards me.

Princess Naghmeh straightened, placing her hand over her heart. "My apologies. It seems I have misunderstood the situation. Please follow me. I will bring you to the Shah." She pointed at Kasabian, eyes simmering with the promise of wrath. "I will deal with you later." She paused to glance at the animals in our company before turning on her heel and sauntered off.

We followed after the princess, her swaying hips accentuated by the draping of her gown. As we walked, I couldn't help but gawk at the astounding vastness of the palace. The ceiling appeared as high as a mountain, and there were green courtyards sprinkled throughout, fountains peeking through the entryways we walked past. We came to a set of burgundy doors, carved with twelve animals.

Kas leaned towards me and whispered, "They're the twelve royal houses of Percia."

I didn't have time to think about the carvings as the guards opened the door, a loud creak echoing in the vast hall as we walked into the room.

The Percian thrones were made out of gold, ornate and intricate. On the larger throne sat the Shah, round belly and a dark-brown, pointed beard that matched his shoulder length hair. On his head was a strange headpiece, as if the bottom of a large, bejeweled bowl had been cut out in order to place it on his head. It looked rather heavy in comparison to the crowns used in Racour: towering and thin strips of gold attached to a circular piece. Most of the queens used ornate hairpins on a daily basis, saving the crown for special occasions.

Next to him was his queen, a willowy woman with brown hair, who had more adornment than her daughter. I knew Percia was the largest importer of gold, but seeing it all displayed was shocking. The queen's eyes were surrounded with black cosmetics, and her lips were colored a dark red. Her hands were covered in jewels, but the skin was also stained a dark brown deeper than her skin, the designs creating floral patterns.

"It's called *hinna*. Women in Percia use it for beautification," Kas explained, catching my stare.

Racourian women preferred adorning their hair in a multitude of pins and styles, as well as pretty patterns sewn on their garments, but they didn't often use jewelry on their arms or necks. Any cosmetics were applied to the face but never the arms or hands.

The Shah spoke with a deep and booming voice, "Welcome! I wish you had informed us of your intentions to visit, Queen Valine. Unfortunately, we are unable to prepare a proper feast on such short notice."

I glanced to the side of the dais where one of the guards from the entrance was scurrying back out. Apparently we had taken the scenic route here.

I bowed my head. "No, I must apologize for my lack of communication. Our plans were made with haste, and thus I had improperly failed to inform the Shah of our visit."

He spread his thick arms wide. "Well I hope you will enjoy your stay, ill-planned or not."

I glanced at Kasabian, hoping he would warn me if I was ignorant of any important Percian custom, but he said nothing, shoulders hunched inwards in an uncharacteristic show of deference. "I do have a favor to ask, Great Shah. I know that the historical records and libraries of Percia are unparalleled in Saego. I have information I am seeking."

The Shah inclined his head. "Ah yes, my guard informed me that you came in order to utilize our vast knowledge." He motioned with his hand, and a girl, maybe only seventeen judging by her young looking face, came forward. She was shorter and less adorned than Princess Naghmeh, although their dark braids and round eyes were the same.

"This is my youngest daughter Vashti. She has an affinity for books and spends her time with her nose stuck in one. She will be able to help you. She is fluent in Ebocian and Racourian."

I nodded in thanks. "I am grateful for your assistance."

The Shah clasped his hands together, resting them on his protruding belly. "I am sure you will be exhausted by your hectic journey here, so I will have some servants bring you to your rooms. The might and resources of the Shah are at your disposal, Queen Valine. I look forward to becoming more acquainted with our northwestern neighbors over dinner."

We bowed in farewell, and a servant showed us to our rooms, Princesses Naghmeh and Vashti in tow.

When we arrived at our respective accommodations, Kasabian was immediately berated by Princess Naghmeh, and I left him to navigate her scorn, entering my designated room with Dryden—heavy panting never ceasing since we arrived—and the dragons. Princess Vashti followed us inside, and, after confirming the safety of the room, Citadel left for his own.

Princess Vashti, cheeks still round with the plumpness of youth, wrung her hands. Her eyes drifted anywhere except my own, although they often rested on the dragons and ice leopard in fascination, constantly studying them.

Sol sniffed the perimeter of the marble tiled room, and Bahm bounced on the purple silk covered bed like a giddy child, the white canopy fluttering from his movements.

Dryden lay at the foot of it, licking the stickiness of the ocean from his fur.

"I suppose you have never seen them before," I said, breaking the silence.

Princess Vashti finally made eye-contact, a smile born of both nerves and excitement on her lips. "Yes. Ice leopards only exist in Racour and Manchur. And dragons... I've read many stories about them, although they are not native to Saego. I'd love to draw a diagram of them for my personal research."

I nodded. "Indeed. I, too, had only heard of them in legends, but wherever my husband's mother was from, they seem to still exist. And you're welcome to draw them, but I recommend doing so from a distance. The green one in particular is a feisty thing."

Sol's violet eyes bore into me through narrow slits as if she understood.

Vashti's brows furrowed, her thumb rubbing against her forefinger. "Perhaps Percia should reintroduce inter-continental travel. It used to be too dangerous to sail between continents, but these days, ships have greatly developed and are better suited to handling longer voyages. It's been a century since a ship came or went. Maybe I could speak to my father..." Her words faded as she drifted into her thoughts, her imagination already taking her to far away lands.

I smiled. "You seem to be a well-learned girl."

Vashti's grin turned wider, and her eyes sparkled. "I have always been curious about things since I was child."

"It's a wonderful trait," I complimented as I set down my things.

My stomach growled, and Princess Vashti covered her mouth, trying not to laugh.

I chuckled. "Would you mind helping me get some food to eat? And then if you don't mind, I would like to head straight to the library."

Princess Vashti obliged, and as we left, I ordered Dryden to watch over Sol and Bahm. He wasn't overly enthusiastic about his task, but agreed nonetheless, nudging my arm with his wet nose before I exited the room.

As soon as we entered the hall, Kasabian slipped out of his room, Princess Naghmeh standing in the doorway with her hands on her hips and her lips downturned.

"Take me with you please," he whispered as his fingers tugged on my sleeve.

"Fine. But you better not use me as a barrier between you and the princess the whole time we are here," I grumbled.

We stopped by the kitchens to grab some cheese and a flatbread that we ate as we walked.

The library was a large, rectangular room with shelves that ran from the floor to the ceiling with ladders sparsely laid against the shelves. The smell of ink, wood, and old paper permeated the air, the sunlight that poured through the tall and narrow windows illuminating the dust particles dancing. There was a rather large area dedicated to Percian laws that Vashti pointed out, and the princess must have noticed my gawking.

Vashti explained as we strode past them, "We have thousands of laws, since a statute, once signed by the Shah, cannot be changed nor revoked, thus if any future ruler wished to, in a sense, amend or remove a law, he would simply make a new decree. Sort of canceling each other out."

"Oh. That sounds... confusing." I muttered.

"So what is it that you are searching for?" she asked.

"Well..." I thought about how much to divulge, but after considering it, I figured there was no point in hiding anything. My voice came out hard, my ice sparking inside me as I explained, "My husband, the Prince Consort, was kidnapped over a month ago. Some pale man with black rocks for teeth and a magic I don't even understand took him." I continued, forcing lightness into my words, "So I suppose anything about creepy men and magic?"

Vashti's mouth hung open as the rest of her body froze. I reached out. "Um... Princess?"

"Well that was not what I was expecting," she expressed. Turning, she walked between rows of shelves and brought me to the section of tomes that included mentions of the first prophet as well as the history of magic. It was a relatively small section compared to the others, yet large enough that it would take me weeks to read every book and scroll.

She reached a hinna covered hand out towards one of the scrolls. Pulling out a cream roll of paper, she unfurled it, revealing frayed edges. In Racour, scrolls were more commonly made of small wooden planks that were bound together with twine, yet in Percia and Eboc, they tended to use parchment. I could appreciate that the parchment took less space, but the durability of the wood made it worth the extra room it took up. Besides, the Racourian characters were able to fit in a small space, while Ebocian and Percian used an elongated script that required more room. Seeing all of them made my chest tighten and my eyes well. Egann had similar looking ones in his tent.

Forcing myself to breath and for the tears to stay put, I cleared the lump from my throat as I stared at the scroll, but it was written in Percian, the lines connecting in undecipherable swirls and curls. I looked up at Vashti. "Would you mind translating it for me?"

She smiled, pumping the balls of her feet up and down. "I would love to!"

She grabbed an armful of other scrolls and handed Kas and I a couple books that had originally been written in Racourian and annotated in Percian. We carried them all to a large table and sat, and Vashti organized the books and scrolls into piles based on their contents. We started with a scroll that was an original copy of the first prophet's words.

We poured over the texts until dinner time, and I sighed, disappointed that we had found nothing of pertinence: a burial ritual, an assassination of a royal from centuries ago, and the methods of meditation according to an old prophet. My exasperation was only increased by my hunger, the flatbread and cheese having long been digested and our stomachs ready for a proper meal.

I was disappointed that we had found no mentions of Noctis or powerful dark beings stealing magic—absolutely nothing related to our current predicament. I leaned forward on the table, my elbows resting between piles of books, and rubbed my temples, attempting to alleviate the headache that often plagued me these days.

A pair of hands started rubbing my shoulders, and I froze.

"I'm just trying to help with a little massage," Kasabian explained.

I turned, eyes glaring, surprised by both his sudden appearance and the physical contact. "If you do that again I'll cut you so you cannot have children."

Kasabian backed away, hands raised.

I stood, brushing past him and gestured for Vashti to lead the way out of the library. We continued to walk through the halls in silence. Princess Vashti looked at me with a mixture of admiration and worry, but she said nothing.

I felt bad for snapping at Kasabian—who was walking behind me with the look of sad puppy—knowing that he meant well, but even if the situation had been different, less serious, I still would not have appreciated the gesture. I only wanted Lux to touch me.

We entered a long and narrow hall, and the smell of lamb, spices, and freshly baked bread wafted into my nose.

Citadel sat cross-legged on top of a purple cushion trimmed in gold with tassels on the corner. Kasabian and I sat closer to the Shah, our stations above Citadel's.

There was a lack of utensils on the table, and I watched, waiting until one of the Percians ate. The Shah started in on his food, using his hands to eat, with the occasional use of flatbread to shovel food into his mouth. I tried to mask the shock on my face. I had eaten with my hands in the past, but it was out of necessity, not having utensils available. A lack of cutlery was not the cause, as this was a choice—a custom.

Princess Vashti leaned over and whispered, "Use your right hand. We use our left hand for personal matters, and our right is thus always for eating."

Intriguing, yes, but such differences in how one ate or even greeted someone was part of what made traveling interesting. Princess Vashti would most likely know about all the details of the cultures in Saego, and my chest tightened, jealousy squeezing my insides that she was afforded the opportunity to study in safety with a stable country and loving family. I had dreamed of adventure as a child, learning languages and receiving an education under the royal tutors, but all that had been stolen from me. My fist tightened, and my nails dug into my palm. I exhaled, expelling the bitterness of all that could have been but wasn't.

Looking around at the array of food, I wondered how things would be in Eboc, my mind then wandering to Zasper. I wished she was with me, but I couldn't handle her judgment, her constant opposition to my choices. I shook my head and reached out towards the rack of lamb, bringing the tender meat to my mouth as the fat ran down my fingers. Juice and flavors of cardamom and turmeric washed over my taste buds.

The queen smiled, creating little crinkles by her eyes. "I take it the food is to your liking, Your Majesty?"

I nodded fervently, forgetting decorum. "Amazing! I'd appreciate it if your cooks could share some recipes for me to take back when we leave."

The Shah answered with a chuckle, "I'll do you one better than that, I'll send one with you. I know of one who has always talked about wanting to visit Racour."

Imitating what I had seen, I placed my hand over my heart and bowed my head. "Thank you."

Leaning over the table, the Shah spoke with a mouthful of rice, "Now, about the reason for your surprise visit, would you mind sharing with us what it is you seek?"

Citadel stiffened beside me, and I knew he wouldn't want me to share the truth behind our coming and would think it unwise to reveal the internal issues of our country to outsiders. But we were at the mercy of their hospitality, and for the sake of efficiency, it was best to be forthright.

"My husband," I paused to clear my throat, ignoring the tension in my chest, "was taken by a man wielding dark magic."

The queen gasped while the Shah dropped the piece of flatbread from his hands.

"I am so sorry," the queen whispered, her eyes watering as her fingers brushed against her husband's arm.

The Shah gently patted his wife's hand. "That must be difficult for Your Majesty. After just having got your kingdom..." He sighed. "Even though we do not share a border, I was aware of Vukan and worried he would bring war to us. When I heard you were alive, I prayed for you, and I thanked The Creator at the news of your successful rebellion."

"It's definitely not how I expected things to happen. I thought the hardest part was over, but it seems like the worst is still to come."

"You're truly inspiring, Queen Valine. I will be praying for you and your husband," the queen whispered, her tear filled eyes glittering in the torchlight.

"Queen Valine always likes to bring the mood down," Kas groaned with a grin.

A tentative chuckle echoed in the room, and we continued our meal with polite conversation.

Eating until I felt like I would burst, I laid a hand on my rounded abdomen. The rice with raisins, garlic flatbread, and fresh vegetables were delightful, and I had eaten more than I originally intended to. But as soon as the meal was over, I was racked with guilt. I was gorging myself on lavish dishes while Lux was suffering, perhaps even being tortured. My full stomach threatened to expel all that I had consumed.

Citadel leaned behind Kasabian's back and asked, "Are you alright, Your Majesty?"

"I think I need to retire for the night," I grumbled.

Citadel stood and came to my side. "Forgive our early departure, my queen is tired from our travels. I will escort her to her rooms," Citadel announced.

The Shah and his queen wished me a speedy recovery, and Princess Vashti stared at me with worry filled eyes while Princess Naghmeh was too transfixed on Kasabian to pay any attention.

We came to my room, and Citadel pulled back the top blanket for me, Bahm and Sol already curled up together on one of the large pillows while Dryden waited at the other side of the bed.

"I didn't realize you were such a good maid," I joked while clutching my stomach.

Citadel didn't laugh. "Please take care of yourself my queen. His Highness would never forgive me if anything happened to you."

I smiled faintly, my eyes and nose beginning to sting. "I'll be fine. So will he."

I tried to convince myself of the last part.

I thanked him for his assistance as he left, the door clicking shut behind him. Dryden hopped onto the bed next to me, and I buried my face into his pelt and tried to rest.

Yet sleep refused me, so I gave up and strode over to the balcony. The weather was warm, but the ocean offered a cool breeze to counter the summer heat. I inhaled, salt and sea filling my nostrils, once again pleasant now that I was no longer on a rocking boat. I couldn't hear Dryden, his soft paws barely making a sound, but I could sense him. On instinct, my hand dropped and buried itself in his fur as I leaned against the sandstone railing, gazing out over the city, the ocean a black mass in the background.

The city was gorgeous in so many ways Pardus wasn't, the roofs flat and angles soft while in most of Racour, buildings were sloped and tapered at the ends while walls created sharp angles. The food, the buildings, the people, all of it was so magical—that sparkling feeling when one discovers something new. But it was dulled by the ache of Lux's absence, and all that came to my mind was how much I wished he were here to see it too. Once I found him, perhaps we could visit all the capitals of Saego, not just Racour, and it would also do good to repair and improve relations that were damaged under Vukan.

You should sleep, Dryden chided.

Glancing down at him, I replied dryly, *That's easier said than done.*

Would you like me to lick you until you fall asleep? he offered. I raised a brow, and he added, *It's what we do to help our cubs fall asleep.*

I couldn't help but laugh. It sounded sticky and wet—completely unpleasant—but was a sweet offer nonetheless.

I'm okay. Thanks.

Dryden sat on his haunches, the sea breeze ruffling his fur.

Do you have a mate? I asked, suddenly curious. He had mentioned Tagon and Kalosa were mates, and that the ice leopards were pairs for life. If he'd had such a pairing already, it must've been incredibly difficult for him to be apart from her.

Dryden's whiskers twitched. *No. I never was able to focus on finding a mate due to the rather irritating and ever pre-sent sense of something missing.* He paused, blue-green eyes glancing at me. *A consequence of not adhering to the blood oath with you.*

I felt a pang in my heart. *Sorry. It is because of me that you don't have a mate.*

Don't feel sorry. I am perfectly satisfied with being by your side.

A smile tugged at my lips. *What do you think would happen if we had never found each other? Would you die?*

Dryden sneezed, or laughed, I wasn't entirely sure which.

I don't know. That aching sensation would plague me my whole life.

And how long is an ice leopard's life? I inquired, shifting and propping myself by my elbow to better look at him.

Similar to a human's. Although if you die, I likely would follow you soon after. Perhaps there were some leopards who outlived their queen, but none that I have heard of.

Then the opposite must also have been true, that if he died I would too. Dying of heartbreak was real, and if I didn't find Lux, I felt like I just might reunite with my mother and friends sooner rather than later. Both of those things were speculation, as both the bond and Lux's status were both filled with unknowns.

We will find him, and you will be okay. He leaned into me. *I will make sure of it.*

After a fruitless day of researching, my certainty was waning. Hope was easy to maintain over a short while, but time had a way of chipping away at it until nothing was left but crushed dreams.

Am I being selfish, for dragging everyone all over the continent? For not being back in Pardus to handle matters of the state?

His whiskers twitched, the thick hairs matching the color of the stars we stared up at. *I think you are very much like our first Glavnyy, who left her position to bond to Constella. Most leopards, myself included, find it an admirable trait. I think that is also why Kalosa chose to help you. As for humans... perhaps they might not agree with your choice. But that's okay. Humans are strange creatures with strange habits.*

Leave it to Dryden to compliment me while insulting all of humanity. I wrapped my arm around his neck. *I'm scared to make the wrong choice, even more scared to lose him. I know we haven't been together long—*

The big cat interrupted, *The length of your relationship is irrelevant. You chose him because he has the qualities you desire, made a choice with your head over your heart. Now if you had chosen that Sebastien... I wouldn't have supported that one.*

I chuckled, *Well I am honored to have approval from the great ice leopard, Dryden.*

In response, he ducked, removing his head from my arm and shifting away, tail drooping and ears flat.

I chased after him and flung myself on top of his back. *Oh, don't sulk. You know I love you. And thanks... for the kind words.*

He twisted and nuzzled my head, his wet nose cold and refreshing against my cheek. *You're the best human there is.*

And you're the best pet cat.

Dryden opened his jaws wide and feigned biting my shoulder, his fangs brushing against my skin.

I giggled. *Alright, alright. I'm sorry.*

We disengaged from each other, and I turned towards the door that led back to the bedroom. *We should try to sleep while we can.*

I better not be in charge of taking care of those dragons tomorrow, Dryden grumbled as we padded inside.

About that...

CHAPTER EIGHT
VALINE

Eager to return to the library and continue searching for answers, I woke up at dawn, dragging Kasabian up out of bed long before he was willing to and leaving Dryden to watch over the dragons much to his chagrin. Thankfully, Kasabian had been clothed when I went into his bedroom, and after a few threats of drenching him in water, he finally got up and got dressed while I waited outside the door. As he exited, my eyes widened, at the sight of him in Percian clothing, a billowing set of golden pants with brown leather sandals on his feet and a red sleeveless tunic that showed off his muscled arms.

Averting my eyes from the caramel hills, I stated with a tone as dry as the desert outside, "You're going to get a sunburn." I crossed my arms, waiting for him to lead us back to the library, as the winding halls were too confusing for me to recall the route we had taken yesterday.

"Well someone is happy this morning," Kas retorted.

"Just start walking," I grumbled, my hand pointing down the corridor.

As Kas led Citadel—who had been present since the moment I stepped foot out my own door—and I through the arching halls, I opened my mouth to ask a question that had stuck to me like tree sap, pestering me until I addressed it.

"How's your face? That was an awfully hard slap by the princess yesterday. I wonder what could have occurred between the two of you to have elicited such a greeting."

Kas yawned, as if the story was as casual as talking about the weather. "We were betrothed to each other from infancy, since my family is one of the royal houses of Percia, and Princess Naghmeh, well obviously she is a princess. As I grew up, I began to resent the fact that everything was decided for me, from the clothes I wore to my future occupation to my marriage. I know I came from such privilege that others could only dream of, but I valued my agency more, yearned for adventure. So I ran away, leaving a note behind and taking nothing with me. Made my way to Racour," he paused to wink, "where I met you."

My mouth dropped open. "Then is this your first time being back? Will you go see your family?"

"I've been back once, for my brother's wedding a few years ago. My mother was elated to see me, but my father... he refused to acknowledge me." Glancing at me, he turned his mouth up in a grin. "Don't worry, sometimes time can soften a hard heart. In one of our more recent letters my mother informed me that my father wished to see me, but then I suddenly had a rebellion to partake in and had to delay coming here. But now you've presented the opportunity for me and an all expenses paid trip home too!"

My father, at least what I could recall, was kind and warm, and I couldn't imagine how a parent could hate their own child. Having seen the scars on Lux's back, I was not ignorant that such parents existed, but I couldn't comprehend such vileness.

Imagining Lux's white and pink lines dotting his back, I quickened my pace, worried about what new wounds he was receiving while we chatted. Before we entered the library, I gently placed my hand on Kasabian's bare arm, the heat of his body warming my cold fingers. "I hope you get to see him, hope you both can reconcile."

Kas placed his hand over mine. "Don't worry we have plenty of time."

My fingers locked together under the warmth from his hands, and I looked up at him, my eyes pinning down his own. "No. You never know how much time we are allotted, so take hold of it, never let an opportunity to spend time with those you love go. Say all that you desire in your heart, or you will end up with regrets."

Without giving him a chance to reply, I tugged my hand free and slipped inside the ornately carved doors and headed to the section of tables. Princess Vashti sat with her eyes trained on a book, teal silks draping in a complimentary contrast to her brown, olive skin. I came up behind her, steps echoing on the tiled floors, and peered over her shoulder, the page she was so intricately studying filled with diagrams of locks and keys and words I couldn't understand.

"Sorry to bother you, Princess, but if you don't mind, I'd like to start researching again." I paused, gesturing to the men behind me. "I brought some help."

She smiled as she replied, taking in Kas and Citadel, "Of course."

She stood and guided us back to the section we were looking at yesterday, pulling down tomes and scrolls and started stacking them in each of our waiting arms. Carrying them back to the table, I explained to Citadel and Kasabian what to keep a lookout for: mentions of murders and missing people or anything relating to magic in general. Kasabian and Citadel began pouring through books in Percian and Ebocian respectively, and I wondered how Lux had managed to acquire such a loyal and skilled soldier.

When my vision blurred and my neck ached from being hunched over, I would take breaks, talking with Vashti about her plethora of knowledge and about Percia's culture and history. She was a walking vault of information; at such a young age she knew three languages and the accompanying history of their countries. She knew about Racour better than I did, Vukan having stolen the years I would have spent receiving an education.

"Did you know that Racour used to celebrate a different holiday to mark the new year? Apparently, they followed a different calendar, but then they shifted to celebrating the same day as the rest of Saego."

I chuckled. "Is there anything you don't know?"

She thought for a moment before answering, "Dubali. But that's because they don't allow any emigration or immigration, so there isn't anyone who can really teach me the language. We only have a few books about them, and who knows how accurate they are."

Vukan's failed war with them didn't help with any potential opening of their borders.

"Your knowledge is astounding, and your mind is incredible."

Vashti looked down at her hands, tracing the floral hinna patterns. "I wish I was beautiful like my sisters."

"What?" I asked, astonished. I was unsure of what was deemed beautiful in Percia, but her plump lips and soft face with hooded eyes would have been the epitome of beauty in Racour.

"My eldest sister, Princess Rebekka, was so beautiful that she had several suitors by the time she was my age. She married the wealthiest merchant in Percia. And Naghmeh too. She was engaged to Kasabian from a young age," she said, her voice absent from its usual confidence.

"Kasabian did run away from their engagement though," I reminded her.

She giggled. "That is a good point." But the jovial expression didn't last long. "But no one has ever expressed interest in me. My face is not as pretty as Rebekka's nor is my body as voluptuous as Naghmeh. I'm just plain in comparison," she sighed.

I patted her back. "Comparison is the thief of joy. Besides, looks fade eventually, but a kind heart and a knowledgeable mind will stay with you. It's always best to find intrinsic value—not depend on others' estimation of your worth—then no one can take that from you. And that confidence will attract a man who finds you lovely inside and out."

She looked up at me, tawny eyes hopeful. "You really think so?"

I smiled and reached out to squeeze her arm. "Yes. There are so many people in the world. You just have to be patient until you find the right one who can appreciate and cherish you. Just don't force yourself into a relationship because you are lonely or yearn to feel desired. Make such a choice out of love and mutual respect."

Vashti sniffled. "Thank you."

I shrugged, my hand dropping to my side. "But it is also okay to never get married. Being single allows you to have a different kind of freedom and the ability to pursue all your passions and hobbies."

She shifted, eyes falling to the floor. "That may be so in Racour, but here in Percia, marriage is an expectation for every citizen."

I rubbed my fingers against my collar bone. "Hmm... Well it is easier said than done to go against customs. I hope that at the very least, you can appreciate the gifts The Creator has granted you. Being humble doesn't equate to being mean to yourself, so learn to appreciate the skills He has developed in you and use them to help others."

Vashti shook her head up and down as she threw her arms around me.

I smiled and patted her head. "Shall we get back to research?" I suggested.

As we went to check on Kasabian and Citadel's progress, my heart leapt and hope sparked when Citadel said he found something that was potentially pertinent.

"Here is a copy of a letter from an Ebocian village leader to the king," Citadel explained, showing me a tan paper with curled and fraying edges. "Five people have gone missing in the past month, including our only magic wielder. The next village over has also been losing members. We found one body near the base of the mountains, and it was horrific. The poor woman's teeth were all missing, and there were cuts all along her arms. We request that the king send officials to investigate the matter."

I chewed on my thumbnail, my mind trying to decipher how it related to Noctis. "I am not sure exactly what it implies, but let's see what Kas had found first."

As I walked around the table, I shook my head in an attempt to ease the internal pressure. So many headaches... Must've been due to the stress. Kas was leaning over a scroll, one finger tracing the text.

"Find anything—"

"Shh!" he hissed, holding up his other finger.

Rolling my eyes, I bit my cheek to keep from replying. My foot tapped against the tiled floor, my gaze following his finger to watch his progress. After what felt like an eternity, his forefinger finally reached the end of the last line.

Leaning back in the chair, he spoke, "It's... almost like a poem. A scorned one. A dark one. Everything is convoluted in metaphors. There was some sort of divine animosity, and the writer speaks of an entity being cast out of the heavens."

Bouncing up and down with her hand in the air, Vashti exclaimed, "I know what it's referencing!" She skipped around the table to us, peering at the document. "It's the tale of The Creator banishing the Dark One from His realm. The Dark One is the antithesis of our Creator, although a much inferior adversary, still bound to obey the will of the Creator to some extent, although it doesn't stop him from trying to overthrow The Creator."

"My father mentioned the Dark One when I was young, although the details are hazy," I muttered.

I flinched as Vashti shoved a book in front of me, pointing to a page I couldn't even read. "I also found this!"

I turned my head, eyebrow raised and eyes darting between her and the page.

"Oh, right," she mumbled, bringing the book back in front of her chest. "It is a chronicle of Eboc. There is this word here: *kivuli*. It keeps coming up in reference to a group who is believed to be connected to mass disappearances and murders a few centuries ago, but suddenly," she paused, flipping to the next page, "they are never mentioned again."

Although it was difficult to analyze everything with my head hurting, I filed the information in my mind and went back to the shelves. My eyes ran over the books and scrolls, hoping to find a title in Racourian so that I wouldn't have to rely on the others to translate for me.

A small thud sounded from the corner. There was nothing on the ground aside from a faded, fraying scroll. I picked it up, careful not to cause any damage to the fragile parchment.

I slowly unfurled it, revealing a long script with an ink painted picture in the corner. The image was of a shadow like monster, black teeth and sharp, pointy fingers reaching out from the page.

"Where did you find that?"

I jumped, almost dropping it.

An apologetic Vashti stood behind me. "Sorry, I didn't mean to scare you. I just have never seen that before."

"I was just standing here when all of a sudden it fell to the floor," I explained.

Vashti held out her hand, and I gave her the parchment. She opened it, and as she read her eyes widened.

She looked up, eyes sparkling. "We found something."

We rushed over to the table and called Kasabian and Citadel over to our side.

As Kasabian read aloud in Percian, Vashti translated.

From the Prophet Isar, son of Abaram, written during the Great Calamity.

Famine, pestilence, and darkness abound. Men and women across Saego are going missing. Some are found, mangled and mutilated, others forever gone. Wails and mourning fill the air across nations. The Creator has revealed our great adversary. His goal is destruction and perversion. He seeks to destroy, the opposite to our own mighty and merciful Creator. The Creator will bind him for four-hundred years, and then he shall arise once more. Only the faith of the chosen few will be able to cast him from our world. I pray that these chosen be strong and courageous, for their calling is full of suffering and sacrifice. But the Creator has assured, that even if they refuse their mission, He shall provide deliverance in others. Peace be with you, you few brave men and women who have been called according to the purposes of Him.

"That's it?" I asked.

"Who are these chosen?" Citadel asked in tandem.

Kasabian turned the scroll over, revealing five images.

A wolf. A flower. A falcon. A horse. An ice leopard.

We gasped collectively. It didn't need to be stated what the ice leopard and wolf symbols meant, and a stone sank in my stomach.

"Who are the flower, horse, and falcon?" I wondered aloud.

Citadel replied, "My family's crest is the horse."

"I think now is a good time to tell you Valine that my house's insignia is," Kas paused, dread weighing down his words, "the falcon."

I'd learned more about Kasabian in one day than the months we had spent together. "What about the flower?" I asked.

"The flower is a Saffron Crocus. It is my birth flower," Princess Vashti whispered.

"What does this mean? Are they, these Fallen, the ones who took His Highness?" Citadel asked, his brows drawn together.

"What should we do?" Vashti squeaked.

My face squished together as I contemplated what everything meant, how it all related, and what our next actions should be.

"Well," I began, "if this prophecy is true—"

Vashti interrupted, much to my surprise, "It has to be! We have librarians that meticulously authenticate everything before it is placed here.

Citadel grumbled, "Well why didn't we just ask one of them about things mentioning magic and shadow people?"

Her face turned red as she stuttered, "Well, they don't always remember everything. They're more like gatekeepers than anything."

I batted my hand in the air, my tone sharp. "Enough. It doesn't matter. We have an idea of who Noctis is now, and we know what our next step is."

"Care to fill us in?" Kas groaned.

"Eboc was mentioned multiple times, so I think we need to go back to Pardus and talk to Zasper. Maybe she knows something about this specific time in their history." I sighed, staring at Vashti, my fingers tapping against my forearm. "But before that we have another favor to ask of the Shah."

No," the Shah bellowed. "You are not taking my youngest daughter on your mission, no matter what some scroll says."

Vashti pleaded, palms plastered together in front of her, "Please, father, I will be of age in a couple months. Besides, the scroll contains the inspired words of a prophet."

The Shah slammed his fists on the arms of the throne. "I said *no.*"

The queen placed her hand on her husband's arm. "Darling, if it is *His* will, then we must—"

The Shah jerked his arm away. "I don't care. She has never left the country, has only even left Terran a handful of times. I will not risk my daughter's life." His voice was calm but full of warning, of looming consequences. "I believe it is time for you to return to your own country, Queen Valine. I will have a ship prepared for your departure tomorrow morning."

Stepping forward, hands in surrender, I begged him, "Please, Great Shah, this is something that affects Percia too. This group, the Fallen, are a threat to everyone. They already rampaged through Eboc centuries ago, and now that they're back, they could attack any country on Saego. Please, you must—"

The booming voice of The Shah cut me off like a executioner's blade, "If they, whoever *they* are, come to Percia, then we shall deal with them at that time, but my daughter is not some pawn just for you to get your consort back."

My hands curled into tight fists, and my jaw was clenched hard enough to crack a walnut. This was so much more than about Lux—of course, he was a big reason–but the potential danger the Fallen imposed was great enough to threaten all of Saego. We knew so little still, but they had killed hundreds in Eboc and who knew what they were capable of now. At the very least they were able to kidnap and keep a man like Lux captive, able to sneak into my court and evade my magic. Why couldn't The Shah see that? And if the cryptic prophecy held the key to defeating them, then we needed Vashti, needed all five of us. I wasn't sure what was required of us, why it needed to be us, but I wanted to follow the words written in order to give us the greatest chance of success.

In my short life, I had experienced the divine intervention of The Creator, saw how He brought people together for His plans. For us to all be gathered together at the same time, for some long-forgotten scroll to appear at just the right time... It had to mean something.

The ways of The Creator were supposed to be the foundation of Percia, and yet here The Shah was ignoring His words. I opened my mouth to say something, to say anything to convince the Shah, but Kasabian grabbed my arm, shaking his head.

Fists tightened into a ball, and teeth gritted, I muttered, "I appreciate your hospitality during this time, Great Shah." Giving a shallow bow, I turned on my heel and left the room, the queen's sympathetic gaze following us and the Shah's ire burning into our backs.

As we walked towards our rooms to prepare for our hasty departure, a hand wrapped around my arm, and I spun around.

Vashti had tears in her eyes. "I am sorry," she whispered.

I patted her hand, unable to meet her gaze for fear that she would easily read the clear disappointment on my face. "It's okay. I understand a father protecting his precious daughter."

Vashti grabbed my hand, jerking me forward. "Since we only have today left, we should go back to the library and find out what we can."

She was right. I couldn't change the Shah's mind, so I might as well make the use of the time we had left here.

I nodded and followed after the princess. She was tenacious in her own way, and strength wasn't always physical. Her mind was as sharp as a blade and her wealth of knowledge was worth just as much as physical prowess. She was capable and strong in a different way from Zasper and myself.

I relied on my physical strength and military skills, while Zasper was cunning and equally skilled with a staff and bows. Vashti had no fighting skills from what I could see by the lack of calloused skin on her hands and from the little I had gleaned about the culture since being here, but I was confident that she could plan her way out of any trouble. I would miss her, and had we been allowed the time, would have become great friends.

Heading to the section of shelves that had held the scroll of Isar, we looked through other works written by him and scanned books for mentions of the Fallen. During one of our breaks, I realized I had forgotten about Dryden and the dragons. I knew the Shah had ordered for the servants to bring them meat and water, but I had failed to inform them of what we had discovered and our unexpected early departure.

Even though the palace was rather large, I was still close enough to get a message to Dryden.

How is everything there? I asked.

I'm going to eat the blue one and sit on the green one, Dryden grumbled.

Just a little while longer. We will be leaving earlier than expected. In a few days when we are back in Racour, you can go hunting.

For a few breaths, there was no reply.

Fine. But in the future, you better not leave me to watch over them.

I chuckled to myself before responding, *Alright. This is the last time.*

I knew he felt neglected and was tired of being on dragon duty, but it was enough to appease him for the time being.

I returned my focus to the books and scrolls, trying to decode and devour as many as I could before we had to leave, my fingers tearing through pages and my eyes ravishing the text.

I'm coming Lux. Hold on.

CHAPTER NINE

LUX

I **_wasn't sure how_** much time had passed. Hours? Days? Months? Without any light, I couldn't even mark the bottom of the cage to try to keep track. And the creature would visit me randomly, so there wasn't a schedule I could work out. Or maybe I was losing it. All I knew was that he would give me some near rancid meat and moldy bread with bitter water, and I had no idea if it was poisoned or not. I'd held out for awhile, but if I continued to not eat, I would die.

I couldn't die. I had to see Valine again.

So I forced the disgusting food down. I had to endure just a little while longer. Valine would come for me. I was certain. Or was I?

Had she already moved on? Had she never really loved me in the first place? Was I just a tool for her to win back her kingdom? She did give the Wulfric land to that pirate. Maybe she intended to marry him.

No.

I couldn't think like that. Our love was real, even if our marriage was arranged. I knew what she was willing to do for those she cared about. Our connection was real. It had to be.

The scraping of something sharp against stone signaled the approach of the creature. "Oh little wolf cub, I have a tantalizing tidbit of information for you," it crowed.

I said nothing.

"Your little queen went on a trip to Percia with that pirate king. Looks like she has forgotten all about you," it sneered.

Lies. They were all lies.

But hadn't I thought the same thing just moments ago? Perhaps they weren't lies. Perhaps it was a deep truth that I was refusing to admit.

No.

Maybe.

It sneered, "Didn't I tell you she wasn't coming? She is just a whore. She lusts for men and power."

If I had the strength I would have slammed my hands against the cage. If only I could access my fire I would have burned the thing to a crisp, but I was gradually weakening and my body didn't want to move.

"Don't talk about my wife like that," I croaked. My voice sounded feeble, but it was all I could muster, the only way I could defend her. How useless I was...

The creature snarled, "You will come to the realization soon enough. After all, who could love the son of a killer?"

My whispered prayers began to grow as did the creature's hisses of pain, as it always did when I spoke to The Creator.

Prayer became a habit, a lifeline, my only weapon against it. At times I felt too weak to even speak aloud words, allowing the doubts to reign over faith—both in The Creator and Valine.

I believed in The Creator as a child, even praying often with my mother. After she died, anytime my father saw me with hands palms up and eyes closed, he would become enraged. My prayers were drowned out by his shouts and my devotion shattered with the vases that flew at my head.

For a while, I had forgotten about Him, as I felt He had me. But that day that dust-covered princess was brought into the court, I began to think about The Creator again. He had kept her and myself safe, and both of us, despite my father, were still alive. The fight in her eyes had relit the fire in me.

Thus the once dormant habit sprang to life due to the tumultuous time of those seasons. In this current predicament, it was even more vital, and a shadow of a smile danced on my lips as the sound of the creature retreating echoed in the cavern.

CHAPTER TEN
VALINE

W_e prepared to board_ the ship that would take us back to Kenobi, the breeze blowing in farewell. The sun reflected off the ocean, the heat causing me to sweat. The absence of the Shah spoke loudly of his dissatisfaction, and I prayed our disagreement would not affect the future relationship between our two countries. It also appeared that I would not be getting that Percian chef.

The queen, iridescent in violet silks and gold bangles, approached with a sympathetic smile. Grabbing my shoulders, she kissed each of my cheeks. "My apologies on behalf of my husband. He can be... stubborn at times. Don't worry though, he will cool off."

I opened my mouth to inquire about the possibility of Princess Vashti accompanying us, but thought better of it. "I didn't mean to offend him, and please pass on my gratitude for the hospitality," I said, placing my hand over my heart.

"Of course. May The Creator bless your journey," the queen said with a smile before turning and walking back to the castle, a trail of guards following.

My body froze as Vashti embraced me with a tight squeeze.

I untangled one arm from her grip and patted her soft hair. "After I get my husband back, I'd love to come back for a visit. Kasabian told me the night bazaar in Terran is spectacular."

She lifted her head, eyes shining. "Promise?"

"Promise," I replied with a chuckle. "We better get going now."

I walked towards the dock where Princess Naghmeh kissed Kasabian's cheek, and they shared a few soft words before parting. Their relationship seemed to have at least developed into something more cordial, perhaps even affectionate.

Suddenly, Bahm darted in front of me, his long tail tangling with my legs, and I fell face first into the sand.

"Well that was very un-royal of you," Kasabian teased. "I wonder what hurts more, your pride or your face?" he quipped.

I spat sand from my mouth. "Shut up."

I stood up and brushed my clothes and face off. I glared at the blue dragon who was hiding behind Dryden's thick forelegs.

Can I eat him now?

No, Dryden.

I stalked past everyone and got onto the ship.

We settled our things below deck, and I prepared myself for two days of sea sickness, as the way to Kenobi was longer than the way to Terran due to the ocean currents. Sitting on my cot chewing mint leaves, I wished we could have just ridden back to Kenobi, but it would have added at least a week to our travels. Lux couldn't afford another week.

Was this how my mother had felt? Overwhelmed by being pulled in a multitude of directions, a mass of responsibilities wearing her down? Perhaps I was too harsh on her; I never really knew the extent of what she went through. The possibility that she wasn't as bad as the people thought, as *I'd* thought, was as shocking as seeing Dryden allow Bahm to lay next to him. My mother could've been a bad queen, or she could have just had a bad reputation. As a child, I had little understanding of court affairs, only having the opinions of others to go off of. I wasn't certain which was the reality, but then again, reality was subjective to the person experiencing it.

What did they think of me? The queen, who just after usurping the throne, abandoned it. I knew very well that I had a duty to the people of Racour, but I had an equal one to my husband. I felt like I would be torn apart by the two.

I shook my head, the thoughts flinging away like water droplets, and steeled myself for a vomit filled day, praying I would be able to sleep through most of it.

As I laid in my cot, my eyes grew heavy, the sound of Dryden grooming himself lulling me to sleep, and I welcomed the sweet relief that slumber would bring.

Heads on spikes were set in a circle. Each face frozen in horror filled expressions. Sokah. Yanish. Egann.

I couldn't tear my eyes from their pained faces. In the center was a rusted cage with an emaciated body laying on the bottom. Lux peered at me through greasy hair, face haggard and dull eyes. There was not an ounce of fat or muscle on his body, his skin clinging to his bones.

I yearned to reach out to him, but my body refused to move.

His voice was hoarse as he spoke, his words full not of accusation but hurt, "Why didn't you come for me?"

Tears threatened to choke me. "I-I am coming. I didn't forget about our promise."

"You let this happen. You're a liar."

"No!" I tried to step towards him, but nothing happened.

I bolted upright, sweat dripping down my back, not entirely caused from the summer heat.

"Are you okay?" a voice asked.

I whipped my head in the direction of the sound. A russet skinned girl with flower stains on her hands sat on the cot across from me, lacking the gold adornments and floral scents that had been present in the castle.

"What are you doing here?" I asked.

Princess Vashti sheepishly answered, fingers dancing with each other, "I-I wanted to help."

I rubbed my temples, a headache forming, which only furthered the harshness of my tone, my words clipped and sharp as a blade. "You can't be here. Your father forbade it. He could claim we kidnapped a princess of Percia and start a war with Racour."

Vashti waved her hands in front of herself, eyes wide. "He would never—"

"You can't be certain! You don't understand what your actions have caused!" I snapped.

The princess folded into herself, and it was hard to tell in the dim light, but I thought I saw tears.

I sighed and put my face into my hands. "I'm sorry I lost my temper. It's admirable that you are willing to pursue an unknown future and participate in a dangerous mission."

Vashti sniffled, wiping her nose with her arm. "I forgive you."

I leaned back against the ship wall. "Well, we are too far away from Percia to turn back now. I will send word to the Shah that you are safe and send you back to Percia once we arrive in Kenobi."

"What? No. You can't," Vashti pleaded. "I know I disobeyed my father, but it was in order to fulfill The Creator's calling. Isn't that more important? Besides, you said I should use the skills I have to help others!"

I wasn't surprised that her argument was convincing, and she was clever enough to use my own words against me. However, I was surprised with my own answer, the words coming out before logic had a chance to take root. "Very well. I won't force you to go back to Percia." The corner of my mouth turned upwards. "Besides, you would just sneak around and follow us anyways."

Vashti beamed. "It was easier than I expected, sneaking onto the boat."

"How did you do it?"

She scooted forward, hands moving as if she were retelling some epic tale of an adventure as she explained, "I hid a pack of clothing I bought from a servant behind a palm near the docks, so after we sent you off I slipped away. I changed and waited until you had all boarded before carrying one of the boxes on the deck onto the ship. No one questioned me. Turns out if you walk with purpose, people assume you're meant to be there."

I had to admit it was brave and clever. As I laid back down, I prayed that I wouldn't regret allowing the Percian princess to join us. I couldn't handle another war so soon, nor could I fight with Percia while looking for Lux.

I popped another mint leaf into my mouth. "You better sleep princess. Life outside the palace is more tiring than you could ever imagine."

Vashti obeyed and laid down, but her feet kept bouncing on the end of the cot.

We reached Kenobi uneventfully and with minimal vomiting from myself. Princess Vashti, now clad in an extra pair of Racourian clothes thanks to Citadel, had taken it surprisingly well, despite having only ridden a ship a few times as a child. I was envious of her strong constitution. For once something was working in our favor, as the distance was too far for a messenger bird, and no boat was fast enough to catch up with us. We had at least a day before the Shah would be able to send someone to Kenobi, if he'd even realized his daughter was gone. However, that meant we had to depart immediately, and I was all too happy at the prospect of riding a horse again now that my sores had scabbed.

Once we reached the inn that housed our horses, I ran to the stables, eager to see Tempest. The gray gelding ate out of a bag of oats. When I approached, his head whipped up. He snorted, lips flapping as I rubbed the soft area around his mouth and gave him a kiss between his nostrils.

You never greeted me that enthusiastically, Dryden grumbled.

Did you forget the time I tackled you out of excitement?

His ears twitched. *That was one time.*

Are you saying you want a kiss on the snout? I asked.

No, he grumbled.

I walked towards him, arms open and lips puckered. *Does the kitty want a kiss?*

Dryden crouched, growling, *Don't call me that.*

I jumped towards him, grabbing the thick fur around his neck, and kissed his forehead. His ears flattened, and he hissed. I backed away laughing.

What? I know you liked it, I giggled.

Just don't call me a kitty again, he mumbled.

Alright, I promise.

He turned his head towards the two Percians. *What are you going to do about her? Won't her sire be upset?*

I nodded. *I'm sure he is irate right now, but that is a problem for future Valine to solve.*

We tacked up our horses ourselves while Kas gave Vashti a brief lesson in wagon driving. Persian women never rode horses, and only commoners rode camels, at least that was what Vashti had said. We needed to be quick, and we didn't have time for her to learn how to ride a horse. It was much easier for her to learn how to steer a wagon.

We traveled back to Pardus as swiftly as possible. The end of summer was marked with heavy rains, which would cause the ground to muddy and an ever present possibility of flooding. We had to beat the storms or we would be delayed even more.

When we stopped for breaks, Dryden would play with Bahm, chasing the small dragon around as I watched with a smirk from afar. Since they rode in the wagon, they had the most energy while the rest of us were tired with sore legs, albeit less so than the first time. We maintained a good pace, following the same trails as before.

With only three days left until we reached Pardus, we decided to make camp early for the night. Princess Vashti had back pain from sitting on the wagon and needed a longer rest. Dryden went off to hunt, and Kasabian kept an eye on Bahm in order to prevent him from following the leopard. Citadel left to forage for berries and roots, having learned what plants were edible during his many dispatches.

I sat on my roll next to Vashti, who was stretching out her legs and back.

"How are you holding up?" I asked while rubbing my chest with a wince. Dryden must have wandered far for his hunt, and I was amazed he could focus on stalking prey with the aching increasing in my heart. But we had lived like this for months while he was in the caves and I in the castle.

Vashti rotated her back, a pop sounding. "Ah, that felt good." She turned to me, folding her legs to one side. "I'm fine, just a little sore from the bumpy wagon."

I leaned back on my hands. "You're doing quite well. You've kept up with no complaints."

She looked down, brushing the stray hairs behind her ear. "I just don't want to hold you guys back, don't want to be a burden."

"Is that what you feel like?" I inquired.

She played with her braid, fingers fumbling. "I don't know. I just know I am not fast or strong, and I don't have any practical skills like hunting, foraging or even making a fire."

"I would have none of those either if I had grown up in the palace. All those skills are one of survival, of necessity. If you never learn them, then thank The Creator that you have had a blessed life." The words came out tinged with bitterness. I exhaled, expelling the envy. "But you are never a burden, and your mind is a valuable skill that is a welcomed addition," I said and meant it.

The corners of her mouth lifted up, and I felt a bit better.

"I know I was born into a wealthy life, but I did want to learn those things," she explained. "But such skills are deemed inappropriate for women. Only men are allowed to learn how to fight."

I bit my lip, regretting the brutally honest words I had spoken just moments ago. I had been judgmental, too quick to make assumptions instead of asking questions. It was strange though, that she wasn't allowed to learn about weaponry, even some basic self defense methods. Most royals learned them out of necessity, internal and external threats constantly looming. Percia had such strange rules, but that was no fault of hers, neither was the fact that my own family was slaughtered which had led to me developing other survival skills like foraging and hunting. I was happy that she had a loving family and secure life, albeit annoyed that her father didn't allow her to train to fight.

An idea sparked to life.

"Stand up," I instructed as I got up from the ground, brushing dirt from my pants.

She bolted up, and I raised my fists in front of me.

"Follow me. Hands stay at your chin level, while your legs," I paused showing her how to place her feet, the dominant further back and knees bent, before instructing, "should be like this. Shift most of your weight to the balls of your feet so you'll be ready to spring forward, lunge to the side, or run away. Which, just to be clear, should be your first choice. Always run."

Vashti cocked her head and opened her mouth to speak.

I cut her off before she could protest against my advice. "If running isn't an option, then you need to know what to do to not die." I bounced around on my feet and showed her some punches. "The thumb never goes inside your palm, or you'll break it. One hand should always be for guarding when the other is attacking. If your attacker is a man, get his balls. But the heel of your palm up the nose will do damage to anyone."

I whipped my leg up, but stopped it right before my foot made contact with her knee. "If you have to kick, keep to the knee, and hitting the back of it will make them stumble. Go too high and they'll likely grab your leg and immobilize you."

"Next," I explained as I brought my forearm in front of my neck, "if you think someone is going to put you into a chokehold, make sure you get your arm up there so you can breathe. Then with the other, you slam your elbow into their side."

"Lastly," I pointed to the left side of my chest before continuing, "You must protect here at all costs. Arrow or blade, you make sure it doesn't go here. Pivot the point of entry to somewhere else. For example, if you can lunge so that an arrow goes into the right side, you'll likely puncture a lung but at least your heart will be intact."

Vashti nodded enthusiastically as she copied my moves. They weren't the best form, but they would do. They would help keep her alive.

Our session ended as the bushes rustled, and Dryden dragged a deer into our camp, blood dripping and staining his fur a dark red. Vashti looked away, covering her mouth as a copper tang floated in the air. I supposed she only saw animals alive or already cooked and not the raw but necessary step that came in between. She excused herself as I took the carcass from Dryden.

I skinned it with one of my daggers that I kept in my waistband, and pulled out the guts, which the dragons for some reason found delicious and devoured in mere minutes. I gave the two haunches to Dryden, who chewed at them while I cooked the rest on a stick over the fire that Kas had made. Citadel returned soon after with some berries and lotus root he had dug from a pond. We ate heartily, and it was a welcome reprieve from the dried rations we had stocked from Kenobi, although I was wishing we had that Percian chef with us at this moment.

Kasabian remained silent the entire time we ate.

"I have never seen you this quiet since I met you. Except for maybe the one time we got caught drinking the milk wine by the captain," I prodded.

Kasabian refused to make eye-contact, instead staring into the fire as he replied, "Just have a lot on my mind."

I poked him. "You've never been the introspective type, Kas."

He leaned his body away from me. "I guess you don't know me that well."

I frowned. "What's with the attitude?"

Dryden interrupted, *You are usually the moody one.*

I glared at him. *Just eat your deer.*

I shifted towards Kasabian. "Seriously. What's up with you?"

He sighed and covered his face with his hands. "There was something else I found while studying in the library."

I scooted closer, my fingers digging into my legs. "What is it? How could you keep pertinent information from me?"

Kasabian finally glanced at my direction before looking away. He spoke, but it was too soft to hear over the cicadas and fire crackling.

"Speak up. You were a pirate. You're good at being obnoxiously loud." The joke felt awkward leaving my mouth as I attempted to relieve some of the tension. Lux was far better at it than me.

"One of the scrolls mentioned a sacrifice," he mumbled, just loud enough to make out.

My body stiffened. "What kind of sacrifice?"

Kasabian shook his head, fingers clenching his legs to the point it looked painful. "It didn't specify. It was too vague. Just that it involved death."

A sword unsheathed. Citadel drew his weapon and pointed it at Kasabian.

"Why didn't you inform the queen? What are your intentions, *pirate*," the Legate demanded, his voice a low growl.

I motioned with my hand. "Put your sword away."

Citadel ignored my command, eyes solely focused on Kasabian.

"That was an order," I snapped.

Citadel bowed his head and sheathed his blade but kept his hand on his hilt.

"Don't forget that he is no longer a pirate. He is a king of Racour," I scolded.

"Yes, my queen," Citadel replied, but his words sounded insincere.

I rubbed the back of my neck. "Why didn't you tell us sooner, Kas?"

When Kasabian responded, his voice cracked, "Because I am worried it may mean you, Val."

"Me? Why me?"

"Because there were too many metaphors about ice leopards and monarchs in the poem. And there is only one monarchy with any relation to an ice leopard." His wet eyes bore into me, glistening in the firelight.

I gulped, forcing the tightness in my throat to dissipate. "I'm sure... I'm sure the part about death was just a metaphor too." My words sounded unconvincing even to myself.

"But what if it isn't a metaphor?" he whispered.

Vashti broke into the conversation, "It has to be. Even in Percia, we have all heard of the great rebellion and victory Queen Valine had over the Wulfrics. The Creator wouldn't grant such a victory just to require her death, right?"

No one answered.

It was very possible that The Creator would ask such a thing. In the history of Saego, many prophets had died horrible deaths in their service to Him. Obedience to The Creator was not a guarantee of safety and a long life, and we had spent a whole day reading the words and biographies of such prophets. Vashti knew too. We all did.

CHAPTER ELEVEN
Valine

There was not a word shared between us the next few days except for what was absolutely necessary. The mood was somber and a great weight hung on our shoulders like a water-soaked cloak.

During our last night outside, the crickets chirped as the stars twinkled in the night sky. The crackling fire danced, and I leaned forward, grabbing some nearby sticks and tossing them into the greedy flames. They were nothing like the gentle waves Lux could create.

"Your Majesty?" Vashti whispered, breaking me from my thoughts.

"Yes?"

She spoke, gaze downcast and arms wrapped around herself, "Do you think we will all die?"

My fingers curled, digging into my palms. "I am not sure. It is likely that many of us will."

"What do you think they want?" she asked as she crouched next to me.

I forced myself to relax my hands, revealing crescents that matched the moon above us. "Perhaps to lure us in, torture or kill us. Maybe they have some way of stealing magic and want mine."

Vashti's voice was as quiet as a mouse as she wrapped her arms around her legs and said, "I'm not afraid to die. But I am afraid of *how*."

A smile cracked my lips. "That makes two of us." I glanced at her, the fire casting a red glow on her skin. "Do you want to go home?"

She shook her head softly, her fingers scrunching her loose linen pants. "No. I want to stick it out to the end. Besides, my father will never allow me to leave my room once I return. I might as well make the most of this trip."

I nodded and brought my hand in front of my face. I flicked my fingers, and a dragon made of ice formed in the air. As I wiggled them, the ice figure danced, and I saw Vashti's wide eyes and mouth parted in an 'o' out of the corner of my vision. I willed for the crystalline dragon to glide towards her, and she held out her palms, where it landed and curled into a sphere.

"That's incredible," she said with awe, her grip around her legs relaxing.

"That took up only a fraction of my magic," I explained.

I saw her open her mouth, but I anticipated her question and answered, "Don't worry. It takes about a full day to replenish it if I use it all up. This much will only take a few hours."

She nodded, but was already asking another question, her curious nature unwilling to accept anything else than complete comprehension of a subject. "Why do you think He doesn't give everyone magic?"

I shrugged, "I have no idea. I don't understand why or how He does so many things."

Vashti pursed her lips and furrowed her brows as she tried to calculate the solution to her inquiry.

I chuckled. "There are some things we will never know until Paradise, and it can be a lot simpler to just accept that fact rather than fight it."

The princess chewed on her bottom lip, her eyes fixated on the fire.

Standing and brushing ash from my clothes, I said, "Well, while you contemplate the world and all its mysteries, I am going to sleep."

I turned and took a few steps to where my sleeping roll was laid out and lowered myself onto it. But whether it was from the weight of my worries or the rock under my mat that I couldn't seem to find, I was unable to drift to sleep.

The next morning started out equally melancholy. We only had an hour or so until we reached Pardus. Once we arrived, we would have to decide on our next course of action. It was daunting, and the closer we got to the palace, the stronger the sense of doom became.

I won't let you die.

I glanced down at Dryden, who refused to ride in the wagon following Kasabian's revelation. He ran beside Tempest and slept next to me, my skin touching his fur any moment I wasn't on a horse.

There are some things that are out of our control, Dryden.

The big cat snarled, *I will not allow you to die for as long as I draw breath.*

I smiled in order to force the tears to stay put as my chest tightened. *I know.*

It was one of the many things I worried about. Dryden would do anything in his power, kill anyone, even sacrifice himself if it meant protecting me. I would do the same.

Before we had ever met, there had always been the minute feeling of something missing, but once we found each other that feeling subsided and every subsequent meeting had been more difficult to part from. Our connection was comforting but also annoyingly codependent. Did that mean if one of us died so did the other? Even though we had discussed it before, neither of us could be certain. If only the first High Queen Constella had left a guide book to magical bonds with wild animals.

I looked back for a moment, staring at our strange medley of a group.

An ex-pirate. A soldier. A foreign princess. One ice leopard. And two young dragons.

I looked back down at Tempest, his dark gray mane whipping through the air as we galloped.

I could die. We could all die.

I had been faced with death on countless other occasions, but this felt different. I had regained my throne, had power, yet all of it wasn't enough to keep those I loved safe, to protect my people. Even if we all made it through whatever this calling was, there would always be something else—*someone* else—to fight. Sacrificing lives, death itself, would forever be a part of my life.

Tempest whipped his head back, and I flinched, narrowly avoiding getting hit in the face. I hadn't realized how tight I was gripping the reins.

"Sorry, buddy. I'll give you some more slack," I said as I let the reins out.

Kasabian brought his horse next to mine, careful to allow Tempest to remain in the point position. We slowed to a trot.

"What will we do next?" he asked with a husky voice.

I shrugged, careful not to pull the leather straps back lest I get another hit to the head. I'd had more than my fair share of those last year. "Even with the prophecy, we don't know where the Fallen reside. Previous mentions of them were predominately in Eboc, and the country is so huge. It would take forever to find them. If they even still exist. Noctis could be the only remnant, or even entirely separate from them. Whether he is acting alone or a part of something bigger, he will be difficult to deal with."

Kasabian didn't reply for a while, silence hovering between us.

"Perhaps Princess Zasper will know something," he suggested at last.

"That's the whole point. I'm sure she knows about that era in Ebocian history but just didn't realize it had to do with our current adversary, " I retorted.

"I haven't known her for long, but from what I gather, she would be the type of person to keep such information from you if she thought it was for the best. She has been against your search for Lux since the beginning, continuously urging you to stay at court."

I didn't want to think that of my friend, but it wouldn't be out of character for her either. I would have my opportunity to ask her soon enough as we came out of the forest, revealing the outskirts of Pardus.

We traveled along the outside of the city, a small trail on the left between the buildings and mountains in order to prevent any delays the bustling capital might present. We pushed our animals hard the last stretch, flanks heaving and hooves pounding and flinging up soil while the wagon rumbled and swayed. They would have plenty of time to rest before we set out again.

As we approached the walls, shouts echoed and the gate opened with a loud groan. We came to a halt in the front yard of the castle and dismounted, and I patted Tempest's neck, ordering the stable boy to give him extra carrots and oats. Citadel held out a hand, helping Vashti down from the wagon. Bahm bounced up and down in the wagon and bumped into Sol, causing her to snap a mouth full of teeth at him. He darted out of the wagon and hid once again under Dryden's legs. The leopard pushed the dragon a little further beneath, obscuring the scaly creature from sight. I smiled for a moment, my heart warming before I peeled my gaze away.

"Citadel," I called.

The Legate appeared before me, hands by his side.

"Take the dragons to my room and make sure they get something to eat," I instructed.

His brow furrowed, and his jaw clenched. "Your Majesty, I would prefer to remain at your side."

I pointed to Dryden. "He said the same thing. So you can either fight each other to decide who stays by me, or you can do as your queen commanded."

Citadel shifted his feet, eyes darting to the big cat whose mouth was already shaped in a snarl, large fangs promising who would win. The Legate bowed and scooped up Sol, Bahm scrambling to follow as he escorted them inside.

"Your Majesty!" Falchor called, running towards me. His feet skidded to a stop. "I am so glad you are back." He lifted me into a hug, squeezing all the breath from my lungs.

I tapped his back to put me down as I gasped for air. "I expect that sort of thing from Mordris, but not from you, Falchor."

His face reddened as he set me down. Mordris was always bear-hugging everyone, wrapping an arm affectionately around his friends, but Falchor never seemed to enjoy physical touch. I was amazed he was able to make a baby.

He scratched his head. "It's just that, Princess Zasper has been... uh."

Kasabian walked up next to me, crossing his arms and whispered, "I've got to hear this."

Falchor scanned the courtyard, ensuring the Ebocian princess was nowhere in sight. "She is not as pleasant to work with as Your Majesty."

"What could she have done that caused you to say that?" I asked.

Falchor looked away, and his voice was quieter when he explained, "She gave instructions that I know Your Majesty would have opposed. She had the consort's things packed and put away."

A frigid cold blazed through my body, my magic sparking to life as I dug my fingernails into my palms. "You must be mistaken."

I pushed past Falchor and stalked into the castle. Guards saluted me as I passed, and servants bowed, but I ignored them all, making my way to the throne room with a furious haste. I didn't even wait for the guards to open the doors for me. I braced my palms against the wood and shoved them. Icy hand prints remained where my skin had made contact with the door.

Zasper sat on the throne, lost in discussion with Myra and Thaddeus. The two stewards noticed me before Zasper did, quickly running out of the room without a word.

Smart.

My friend noticed me and smiled. She stood and ran down the dais steps towards me. She wrapped me in an embrace, but my arms stayed hanging at my side.

Pulling away, her face looked confused at my lack of an enthusiastic greeting. "What is wrong, *Chui*?"

I stared into her brown eyes, hoping that it wasn't true, but knowing that I had to hear from her myself.

"Did you order Lux's things to be removed and put into storage?" My voice was dark and bitter, ice crackling under my skin.

Zasper stepped back, her hands hanging loosely at her side. "Ah, so you heard. I wanted to tell you myself. I think it is time to put away this futile search. I know you cared for him, but I assure you that with time you will forget about him."

My heartbeat quickened, ice flaring in my veins, and venom filled my words, "I think it's time that Eboc's princess returned home."

"What?" She had the audacity to look shocked. To look hurt.

"Go home, Princess Zasper."

I turned on my heel and left the room.

CHAPTER TWELVE
VALINE

I *strode towards the* mahogany armoire and ripped the doors open. Women's silk tops, the straps of the cloth that secured them around the body dangling loosely like ribbons from the rafters, and voluptuous skirts hung from the bar inside. But there were no men's garments.

Slamming the doors closed, I forced my heaving chest to settle and coaxed my ice into calming.

I had instructed the guards to allow no one to bother me unless it was an emergency, so the sound of someone knocking on my door only served to reignite the icy fire I had just quelled. I sucked in a breath, cocked my head, and curled my fingers into fists, doing my best to contain my irritation.

Want me to kill whoever is on the other side? Dryden asked, ready to pounce.

Maybe, I replied as I stalked towards the entrance.

If it wasn't urgent, I was going to throw whoever was on the other side in prison for disobeying the command of the queen, and as I ripped the door open, I was determined to hold true to my threat. Zasper stood in the entryway, face filled with sorry and sorrow.

My cold wall I had built to sever our friendship melted ever so slightly at the sight of her wringing hands. I pivoted away and walked to my bed. It no longer had the faint scent of Lux, and I was certain Zasper had ordered for the sheets to be replaced. The wall refroze.

"What do you want?" I asked with a frigid steel.

Zasper took a step inside, palms open. "I am sorry."

"That's it?" I spat.

She took another step. "King Armani explained what you discovered in Percia. I didn't realize this was the will of The Creator. If I had known that the wolf was an integral part of a prophecy—"

"Lux. His name is Lux," I reminded her, eyes narrowed.

She bowed her head. "I am sorry."

I crossed my arms. "Are you sorry because you hurt me and dishonored my husband? Or are you sorry because now you feel as though you opposed The Creator's will? Who are you sorry for, really?"

She paused her approach. "Both."

At least she was being honest.

Zasper's voice softened as she spoke, eyes reading my face, "I am sorry for hurting my friend and being only focused on what I thought was good for her that I ignored her feelings. I was being selfish while believing what I had thought was better for you, for Racour." She sighed, hands dropping to her sides. "And now The Creator has shown me how foolish I have been. So, I am sorry."

"I told you I didn't want to give up, that I wouldn't stop searching. I plainly stated to you what I wanted. Why couldn't you respect that?" Grief and anger mixed together in my voice.

Zasper's fingers rubbed against each other, her eyes downcast. "I know. I was wrong. All I can say is I am sorry."

My mind warred with the possibility that it was all a ruse, an empty apology meant to placate me and encourage me to follow the scroll. Zasper had lied as to her purpose in Racour long ago, all as a guise to meet and help me, so I knew she was capable of deception. Staring into her eyes, I couldn't—didn't—want to believe that she would lie to me.

"*Chui*," she whispered, her hand tentatively outstretched yet frozen on her side of an invisible line—an invitation, free to reject or accept.

The wall crumbled and tears filled my eyes.

A clump in my throat formed as I stumbled forward, and we folded into each other, falling to the floor. It was the first time I had seen Zasper cry. I didn't want to lose such a good friend, even when what she did was hurtful. Loyal friends were hard to come by, and sometimes we all made mistakes and needed grace. Including myself. My friends were forgiving even when I pushed them, when I was blind to their fatigue in the search for Lux.

I knew as she apologized and allowed me to see her weep that she was truly sorry. In the end, we were all just doing the best we could.

After sobbing until there were no tears left, we scooted back, wiping the snot and wetness from our faces.

Dryden, who had watched us without a word in my head—allowing us the space to work things out—padded over to us and licked my cheek.

"Hey! I just dried it off," I whined.

In retaliation, Dryden turned and whacked his tail into my head. *Better?*

I shoved him, but he pounced on top of me and began licking my face with the ferocity of a mother cat.

"Dryden!" I squealed, attempting to block his rough and slimy tongue with my forearms, but they, too, were quickly covered in leopard saliva.

"Gross," Zasper commented.

"Want me to get the dragons?" I threatened.

Dryden jumped off and sat far away, paws tucked under himself.

Zasper and I giggled as we stood and went to the bed. I patted the spot next to me, and she sat, sinking into the mattress.

Once more, Zasper's voice returned to its serious state. "Actually, there is something else I need to tell you. It's about the Fallen."

We will go to what was House Stallian's territory under the guise of finding a new king for the region," I informed them.

"What?" was the collective response.

I gestured to Zasper, and she stepped forward to explain. "There are Ebocian legends—stories—usually told to children to make sure they listen to their parents. 'If you don't do your chores the Shadow People will get you.' Things of that nature. But there are tomes deep in the record halls that only the royal family of Eboc has access to. I used to be obsessed with sneaking in to read them as a child."

Kasabian interrupted, "What do children's stories have to do with the prophecy?"

Zasper glared at him. "I was getting to that, King Armani." She let out a breath and continued. "In those locked away books, there are mentions of the Shadow People. Or the Fallen, as you have referred to them. Before Queen Constella and your people arrived, there were decades filled with fear and kidnappings and murder. Until one day a descendant of Abaram came. His name was not recorded, but it was written that he was able to chase them away to the northern hills." She looked around the room of those we had called together. "The hills that were apart of the land granted to Queen Constella, and the lands which she later designated to House Stallian."

Myra, who stood in the back of the council room, gasped. Falchor cursed, and Citadel's brows furrowed, eyes filled with calculations and puzzles.

"Noctis' mouth was filled with obsidian fangs instead of teeth, and his sister had some sort of dark blue gem if I recall correctly. I can't help but wonder about Stallian..." My voice trailed off as I worked to connect everything. "Who knows what lies in the depths of those mines? Perhaps he has been aware of them, even partnered with them. Maybe he was secretly doing things that even Vukan was unaware of."

"Or working with both of them," Zasper suggested.

"That bastard Dumas."

We turned to Thaddeus, shocked by his outburst. He was usually a quiet and gentle-spoken man, only replying when asked a question.

His chubby cheeks reddened, and he bowed. "My apologies, Your Majesty."

I did my best to hold in my laugh, folding my lips inward before replying, "No, no. That's quite alright, Steward Thaddeus."

Dryden was not so successful, and his wheezy chuckle made it harder to hold my own laughter in.

I cleared my throat. "Falchor, any word from Mordris?"

Falchor stood straight. "He has received our message and says that he will return immediately."

I nodded, hand rubbing my chin. "Good. And any response from Raven Bone, Steward Myra?"

She shook her head. "My apologies, my queen. Every messenger we sent to the mountains was unable to locate the Waodani."

I sighed, slumping into my throne. "I'm not surprised. I will need to go to him myself before we depart."

Citadel broke in, "Did you ever inquire if the leopards knew anything?" The Legate glanced at Dryden, who had taken up his position next to me, but ripped his gaze away faster than a frightened rabbit as the big cat snarled.

If I or my clan had any information, we would have shared it. We do not hide things like humans.

I ran my hand through the fur of his neck in an attempt to flatten his raised hackles. "He said they don't know anything about the Fallen."

Princess Vashti spoke next, her voice starting off quiet but growing louder as she continued. "Well, um, I think that we should plan this out more. I know Your Majesty is eager to reunite with your husband, but if this order is as dangerous as we have heard and read, then we need to be careful."

Nods around the room.

It was true. We had no idea what was waiting for us there. An army of dark beings all equally powerful like Noctis? Even Lux, with his fire magic, had been unable to escape this entire time, so they were obviously more powerful than anything we could have imagined.

"Well," I said standing, "I suppose there is no better person for fighting Shadow People than the wielder of shadows."

Raven Bone. Dryden stated.

"Raven Bone," I said aloud for the benefit of the others.

"Will you leave soon, Your Majesty?" the stewards asked in unison.

I smiled sympathetically. "I'm sorry. You two will have to continue to manage things without me for the time being."

They bowed. "It's our honor, Your Majesty."

"Falchor, wait here for Commander Mordris. Once he arrives, join us at Stallian's castle. I will go with Dryden to find the Waodani while Kasabian makes arrangements for our travels. The Legate will prepare a small guard to take with us."

Zasper's face fell. "You're leaving me behind again."

I walked over to my friend, grabbing her hand. "It's not a punishment. I need someone here. Besides, there was no baobab tree symbol in the prophecy."

"There was no mention of an army or Raven Bone either," she pointed out.

I squeezed her hand. "I still need someone here, someone I trust."

She smiled, although it didn't reach her eyes. "Very well."

"The glory is shared both by those on the front lines and those whose support allows them to be there." I released her hand after one more squeeze and turned to the others. "I expect you all to be ready to leave by this evening."

"So much for planning," Vashti whispered.

I chuckled. "For me, this was a good amount of planning ahead."

Kasabian elbowed the princess. "It's true. She is rather impulsive."

A true smile finally formed on Zasper's lips. "I concur."

The mountains were still cool at their tops, even during this time of year. They were covered in short brush and the occasional tree that dared to try to survive in the harsh elevation.

I went to the general location that I remembered meeting the Waodani the last time. Although with the summer terrain, I wasn't entirely sure where that was.

Lost? Dryden sniggered.

No. Just... enjoying the scenery, I retorted.

In reality, Dryden was enjoying it far more than I was. This was part of his realm, where the ice leopards lived and hunted. Every time he found a scent that he found pleasing, he would roll around in it, but I couldn't say the smell was particularly pleasant to humans.

Do you have to keep doing that? I asked, exasperated.

Dryden paused, looking at me upside down, his head still touching the ground and paws in the air. *Do what?*

I waved around. *Whatever that is.*

He flipped over, ears flat. *I've spent so much time around humans that I am beginning to smell like one.*

"Maybe I should try rolling around in the moss and dirt. Maybe I can attract more suitors."

I whipped towards the voice, my hands instinctively withdrawing my blade from its scabbard. Raven Bone stood alone, unaccompanied by Leopard's Bane or any of the other Waodani.

His eyes were covered in a black cloth.

My frustration made me forget my manners. "What's with that thing on your face?"

"Even though my eyes can't see anything, they can still feel pain. The cloth protects them from the sun," he explained. "The first time we met was at night, and the second was during a battle, and a cloth covered face is not exactly intimidating, is it?"

"What about during the coronation?"

He smiled. "I wanted to look handsome for all the pretty ladies."

"Ah, I see," was all I said.

He leaned on his walking stick. "And to what do I owe the pleasure of Saego's most beautiful queen?"

"How can you be so sure I am the most beautiful?" I asked incredulously.

He replied, "Well, have you seen the Manchurian queen?"

"The Manchurians don't allow queens to rule," I said as I rolled my eyes.

"Well then, that helps narrow the competition, doesn't it?" He laughed.

I had to get our conversation on track. "I need your help again."

Raven Bone smirked. "Are you prepared to fight for my assistance again?"

He stepped forward and dropped his stick, twin black blades beginning to form in his hands, but suddenly his feet came out from under him. The ice I had formed on the ground beneath his feet worked as well as I'd intended.

I held out my hand in front of him, "I'll help you up."

"How could you do that to a blind man?" he asked in shock while grabbing my forearm.

As he stood, I willed the ice to melt.

"Are you accusing me of playing dirty tricks?" I asked innocently.

He chuckled. "So fun, little queen!"

I sighed, rubbing the center of my forehead. The headaches were becoming more frequent as of late. "I don't have time for your games, Raven Bone."

He retorted, "You had time when you were starting a rebellion. What's more urgent than that?"

"An order of magical people who are apparently intent on spreading death and destruction and who were able to capture my husband despite his swordsmanship and fire abilities."

All playfulness dropped from his expression, his lips losing their typical upturned position. "Oh. That does sound more serious."

"Have you ever heard of the Fallen or Shadow People?" I asked, my voice filled with hope that perhaps the leader of the ancient people would hold some answers we desperately needed.

He cocked his head. "Did you forget who I am? What power I possess?"

He demonstrated, and a dark cloud enveloped us. Then small shadow figures appeared between us as he narrated the scenes.

"Our oral tradition states that shadow magic was granted to us by The Creator in order that we may protect ourselves. The Waodani leader is always blessed with shadow magic, and only the chosen apprentice to the chief is bestowed with it. Centuries ago, there was a chief who was torn between two apprentices."

Three shadowy figures appeared together in a triangle formation, one hunched over, one towering over the others, and one short but with a straight posture. "One was smarter, stronger, more calculating—objectively he would have been a good choice, except that he was not compassionate. He was too dogmatic and lacked mercy, so the chief of that time chose the one who, although her skills were nothing special, was kinder and wiser. The shadow magic thus went to her, and the other apprentice felt forsaken and underappreciated. In his determination to prove how he was better suited to be chief, he went astray."

A black misty orb appeared in front of the tallest figure. "He dealt with The Dark One, a malevolent entity that belonged to the heavenly realms but was cast out for his own transgressions against The Creator. The scorned apprentice made a blood oath, along the same lines of the one you queens made with the ice leopards. The apprentice was provided a perverted version of the Waodani's shadow magic, but at a great cost."

The tall figure walked up the mountains to where the Waodani lived, but the hunched silhouette from before pointed a finger back down from where the figure came. "He was banished from us, and if the chief then knew what would become of his scorned apprentice, perhaps he would have made a different choice. Perhaps the chief would have tried harder to guide him back—or end the threat then and there. Alas, we cannot change the past, and the following death that was wrought upon Saego was all the work of The Dark One and the apprentice." A shadow village appeared, with fanged figures barging into it, grabbing people and dragging them off.

"It seems that they were forced into hiding for a while, but now they have appeared again."

Had I not been so stressed, I would have enjoyed the dramatic story-telling. Was Noctis the 'Dark One' from the story? Why was everything 'centuries ago'? And why had no one properly resolved the problem before now? Why did I have to handle it? Wasn't ridding the world of Vukan enough? I supposed all the prophets and great rulers of old had felt the same way; the burden of being called to great things was that they also required great effort and hardship. *Sacrifice.* My skin prickled and my body shuddered at the thought of what sacrifice would be required of us.

Was it a small sacrifice from all five of us, the culmination of what we would have to give up the key to defeating these Fallen? Or did only one of us have to bear the burden?

The shadows evaporated and the little shadow people that had been acting out the tale dissolved into nothingness.

"Will you help me once more?" I asked.

Raven Bone stretched out the silence before answering, "I suppose I must. This all started with the Waodani in the first place."

I sighed in relief, my shoulders relaxing. "Thank you. I will fill you in on the way down."

"Carry me?" he asked with arms outstretched.

"Your legs work fine," I grumbled, turning to walk back the way we had come, Dryden bounding around in circles.

"Do you have an apprentice?" I asked, my eyes trained on the trail in front of me lest I trip or roll my ankle.

"No. I am still early into my chiefdom and have plenty of time to pick one."

With the danger I was dragging him into, perhaps he wouldn't have as much time left as he presumed. We could all be going to meet an early demise.

"*Well I didn't see* that coming." Raven Bone laughed at his own joke, the sound echoing and bouncing in the mountains.

"Ha. Ha. Very funny," I muttered, kicking a stone that had the unfortunate luck of being in my path. The small rock tumbled, clacking against other boulders and pebbles on its way down. I resisted the urge to stick my tongue out or make obscene gestures, knowing it was childish and unfair. But I only *just* barely stopped myself.

As we continued our trek, Raven Bone finally allowed himself to be serious about the matter at hand. "So your husband hasn't been able to escape even though he's got that gnarly fire stuff."

I nodded, but then paused mid-movement after realizing he wouldn't be able to see the action anyways. "Yes. Which is concerning. If they can keep him trapped, then what will it take to free him?" I refused to speak, to even think, of an alternative, that Lux was already dead.

Raven Bone deftly worked his way down the mountain, the ties of the cloth covering his eyes tangling around his white hair. "Well, who knows what kind of deals they've made with The Dark One. Perhaps there is some sort of enchantment to keep his magic bound. Wasn't yours bound too? Didn't that old man have to help you?"

I was curious as to how he knew all that in such detail, but my head was aching too much to waste a breath on asking. Instead, I simply answered, "Yes, but don't ask how that all worked because I have no clue. I never seem to know anything that would make things easier."

Raven Bone leapt over a large rock, landing lightly on his feet, his stick clacking against the stone. "I wonder if they were able to imitate the binding on your magic for him? Or perhaps some weird, creepy ritual to block magic inside a room."

"Interesting theory. What makes you say that?"

His voice lowered. "They weren't just killing for the joy of it, they were taking people, mutilating them, twisting them into something dark, something monstrous, and only those who refused to submit, to give themselves over, were ever found. Well, only their bodies. Even the blood was drained from them. Maybe the blood can feed their magic."

I wondered how he knew so much, but I just didn't care, couldn't dredge up the motivation to ask any questions. With my head throbbing, my sole focus was on getting to Lux. Nothing else mattered, not the history, not the prophecy, nothing.

I didn't care what perverse experiments, what evil entities awaited us, I was going to get him back.

CHAPTER THIRTEEN

LUX

Time was irrelevant in the darkness. My muscles atrophied into nothing, my hope fading away with them. The doors could be left open and a path illuminated, and I would still be unable to escape. I figured I would only have the strength to walk a few steps before collapsing.

The energy it took to consume the poor excuse for sustenance was all I had for a day, or what I thought was a day. Bringing the rusted cup to my mouth caused my pulse to quicken and my arms to shake. I could imagine my father's voice full of scorn as he berated me, his weak and pathetic excuse for a son.

My mother still appeared in my dreams, her sweet and soft voice singing, but whenever I looked at her for comfort, the voice was coming from a pale face and bulging eyes, body swinging from the rope in tune with the melody.

"She isn't coming for you," the voice whispered.

I fought the tears rolling down my cheeks. "I know..."

CHAPTER FOURTEEN

VALINE

My *head hurt, and* my body was worn from constant traveling and stress that grated away at me like a river eroding the earth. The headaches were almost daily occurrences, albeit the severity varied day to day. My skull throbbed and the internal pressure on my brain was unbearable at the moment. If I had to hear one more of Raven Bone's jokes, I was going to freeze him. Or myself. Whatever would stop the pounding in my head.

Tempest thankfully had given up his point position, the gray gelding seeming to sense my pain and poor mood. His gate was extra smooth, and he didn't try to race ahead of the group, which also made Citadel happy, as he was always concerned that I would be too easy of a target at the front of our entourage. My fingers twirled his coarse mane as the summer sun bore down on us.

A yelp sounded from someone behind me. Turning my head, I saw Princess Vashti bouncing awkwardly in her saddle as she struggled to maintain her seat as her spooked horse took off. Perhaps we should have kept her in the wagon. Lucky for her, Ferrum—Mordris' nephew—came up beside her, yanking on her reins and bringing her horse to a halt.

"Woah..." he spoke with a soft but firm voice to the horse. He looked at the princess. "Are you alright, Your Highness?"

Vashti tucked her hair behind her ear and lowered her chin. "Yes. Um... Thank you," she mumbled.

Ferrum grinned and handed the reins back to her. "I'll be right behind you, so no need to worry, Princess." He backed his horse into position directly behind hers, and Vashti's lips curled into a faint smile.

I turned my gaze forward, a pang of jealousy stinging my chest. Everywhere I looked I was reminded of Lux, in the soil I found his eyes, in the rustling trees I heard his voice, and every touch of Tempest's mane made me imagine the hair was longer and darker—soft when one ran their fingers through it.

After months wandering all over Racour and even down to Percia and back, our retinue was finally going in the right direction, a certain purpose guiding us onwards. Something within my gut knew that this was the summation of all the pieces we had collected. *I'm coming, Lux. Hold on!*

I lifted my head, my eyes tracing the heavy looking clouds. "Please. You have helped me through so much, so do not abandon me now. Help me find him," I whispered to The Creator, allowing the breeze to carry my pleas all the way to the heavens.

As I fixed my eyes back on the path ahead, something deep within me stirred. It was strange. The closer we got to Venore—the capital of Stallian's region—the quieter it got. No birds chirping in the trees, no rabbits rustling in the bushes, and no deer leaping through the long grass. Something was... *off*.

House Stallian's castle appeared simple on the outside. The roofs were all pointed so the snow wouldn't accumulate and cause a cave in, and the buildings were never more than two floors high since the lower it was, the easier it was to keep heated in brutal northern winters. Trees dotted the terrain, but the hills were the dominant features in the north, mines nestled at their feet.

Despite it being summer, the air was cooler and offered a reprieve from the humid and stifling climate of the southern areas of Racour. The sky darkened, and the clouds held the promise of rain as we stopped outside the gates, my eyes roving over Dumas' residence. His *previous* residence.

An iron wall of pointed spears surrounded his estate instead of wood or stone like the other capitals and major cities. I'd never seen anything like it before. The gaps between the posts were too slender to squeeze through. It was impossible to climb over, as one would be impaled in the attempt, and it couldn't be burnt down like the wooden walls of Manchur or King Koodsin's domain of Sosoni. A metal gate with some sort of lock mechanism was in the middle.

I dismounted, Tempest's nostrils flaring and eyes wide as his hoof stomped into the ground. His ears flattened, and I ran a hand along his neck. "What's wrong, boy? Can you sense something?"

I looked at our entourage. *Dryden, come here.*

The big cat bounded up, leaving flattened grass where his paws hit the ground. Sol and Bahm padded after him, the blue dragon making sure to step in Dryden's pawprints.

Can you smell anything unusual?

Like what? His black nose twitched as he lifted his muzzle to the sky.

I shrugged. *I don't know, but Tempest seems anxious.*

Dryden lowered his head. *You're worried because of a horse?*

Can you pick up anything or not? I demanded.

Dryden's ears flicked forward. *There is something that smells rotten, but it could be anything. Like an animal carcass.*

"Citadel!" I called, waving the Legate over.

He jogged over, sword clanging against his leg. "Your Majesty?"

"Something is strange. There is no one in sight, no servants, no guards," I commented, rubbing the goosebumps on my arm.

The Legate scanned around us through narrowed and focused eyes. "Indeed. Do you think Zasper ordered the premises to be vacated while we were away?" he proposed.

"I think she would have told us if she had. Perhaps without their king, they left of their own accord. On the bright side, it should make it easier to search the estate."

I peered to where Princess Vashti was sloppily dismounting, Ferrum standing behind her with arms at the ready in case she fell.

"Maybe we should leave the princess and some of the men here while the rest of us enter the estate," I suggested.

Citadel followed my line of sight towards the princess. "That sounds like a good idea, Your Majesty."

"Why don't you ask her what she wants to do?" Kasabian walked up beside me, Raven Bone in tow. Kasabian continued, "She knew what she was getting into when she stowed away on that ship. You should give her the option of choosing. That's what brought me to Racour too.

Agency. I wanted to choose my own path and my own partner. I didn't want someone else making the decision for me."

I eyed him. "That was deep coming from you."

Kasabian grinned, a spark igniting in his eyes, displacing his serious expression. "I am as deep as the ocean, Val. You just have to brave the seas to discover it."

I rolled my eyes, but the movement caused a sharp pain to stab in my skull. I hissed, clutching my head. My palms pressed into my forehead, as if I could shove the sensation away. Citadel's fingers rushed to my elbow, and Kasabian placed his hand on my back.

"Val?"

"Your Majesty?"

Scales and fur rubbed against my legs. I removed my hands from my face, a mixture of human and animal eyes looking at me with concern.

Blinking rapidly, the sharp pain subsided, replaced by the dull throb that had plagued me the past couple months since Lux had been taken.

"I'm fine," I forced out. I shook my head, refocusing. "Alright, let's ask the princess what she wants to do."

Clapping thunder echoed and wet drops began to hit us as we walked towards Vashti who was laughing at Ferrum, his face contorted and eyes crossed to elicit such a reaction. Hearing our approach, Ferrum immediately stood straight, face returning to a neutral state at the sight of his sovereign and commanding officer.

Vashti smoothed her clothes and cleared her throat. "Your Majesty, are we not going inside?" She glanced up at the sky that had decided that now was a great time to start a downpour, water quickly turning the dirt to mud as the thundering storm shook the earth as the branches waved from the mighty gales.

A memory crept to the front of my mind, the words of Noctis' sister; something about the ground moving and the skies opening?

Kasabian answered Vashti's question before I could. "That is up to you, Princess. The queen has offered to allow you to stay here with some soldiers while the rest of us enter the premises and ensure it is safe."

The princess squared her shoulders, rain pinning her hair to her face. "Of course I am going with you all." She said it with such resolution that it allowed no room for questioning. At seventeen, she was near the same age I was when my rebel group started looting and doing active missions. She was perfectly capable of making her own decisions, and the dangers had already been exhaustively explained. We all had heard the prophecy, even if we didn't know what exactly it referred to, whatever it was would be difficult and possibly life-ending.

I nodded. "Let's go then."

Citadel pushed on the gate, but it refused to open. Despite pulling and shoving, the metal didn't budge, only shaking with a strange sound that matched the roaring skies.

Removing a small pin from her hair, Vashti stepped forward and stated, "I can open it."

"Impressive," I said as I gestured her towards the gate.

She walked forward, shoulders slumped and teeth chewing her lip. Despite her nerves, I was confident that she would complete this task with ease, even if she didn't share that sentiment.

Her fingers fumbled for a moment, and I assumed that she was keenly aware of all the eyes staring with expectation at her back. After a few moments, her hands steadied and a loud click sounded. She pulled the lock up and off of the gate, the metal creaking as it opened.

We led our horses through on foot. We walked with caution, mud sucking at our feet and the horses' hooves creating craters that filled with water in their wake.

Once we reached the doorway, we were hit with the sickeningly sweet smell of rotten fruit, and a faint buzzing noise emitted from behind the doors.

"I don't need to see to know that whatever is behind that is nasty," Raven Bone said in a nasally voice, pinching his nose between two fingers.

I had heard that blind people developed stronger senses to make up for their loss of sight, although I wasn't sure if that was true or if Raven Bone was just being himself.

I nodded at Citadel, and he instructed two soldiers to open the silver plated doors.

A wave of rancid air swept forward like a gust of wind, and a few flies rushed out of the building and flew into the sky. I gagged, my hand instinctively covering my nose and mouth. The soldiers slammed the doors closed, offering a slight reprieve from the onslaught of the horrid stench. We cut up a spare shirt—doing our best to keep it dry despite the downpour—to cover our faces, and Vashti suggested we rub some soap from our packs on the cloth to help mask the smell.

With our makeshift masks, we opened the doors once again, the scent of rot still noticeable but more tolerable now. We trudged forward into the dimmed halls. No torches were lit, and there wasn't enough natural light to illuminate everything. Shadows clung to the corners with the ceiling obscured in darkness. What I would give to have fire magic like Lux.

While we lit torches, Dryden offered, *I'll go first. I can see better than your human eyes can.*

I lifted an arm, knowing that they could smell better too. *After you.*

The big cat padded inside, his soft paws near silent on the marble floors, and we followed, our wet shoes squelching, the now lit torches in the soldiers hands providing enough light that we wouldn't be surprised by anything.

The walls were painted white, an uncommon color, usually only used by the wealthy who could afford to maintain it and keep it clean, and paintings and jeweled vases were on display along the corridor. It looked like Dumas had been skimming from the mines.

"Should we be trying to find the source of the smell or move away from it?" Raven Bone asked.

Citadel replied, "As much as my nose abhors it, we should go towards it."

Kasabian nodded in agreement. "In all my days of being around men who haven't showered in weeks, this is the worst stench I've experienced."

Princess Vashti coughed as she asked, "What could be making this smell?"

We would have to keep moving in order to find out.

After hours spent combing the eerily empty building, we still couldn't find the source. There was however, an area of the castle in which the smell was the strongest. In what we assumed was Dumas' living quarters—an obstinate and obnoxiously decorated area—the stench was the most rancid, and the dragons were reluctant to enter the room. Raven Bone also had to take breaks and go outside to cleanse his nostrils.

Citadel gagged as he reached for the doors. "Not enough soap in the world to mask this stench."

Kasabian looked at me with a half-smile. "Is there magic that can make perfume?"

I shook my head, regretting it as soon as I moved, the throbbing in my head increasing. "I wish, but I doubt it."

Ferrum interjected, eyes glancing towards Vashti and shoulders extra straight, "I'll go in first." He moved towards the door, but even the mask couldn't hide the expression his eyes made as the smell infected his nose. His eyes crinkled, but he endured, suppressing a gag. Vashti stared at his back, eyes sparkling.

As the door clicked open, the soft buzzing that had been present the entire time we had been in the castle roared to a cacophony. A storm of bugs flew out of the room in a black cloud, buzzing wings filled my ears as we slammed our eyes shut. I ducked down, covering my head with my arms as they refused to leave us alone, continuing to fly around in an unending barrage. I conjured ice and willed it to freeze the bugs, and one by one they fell with the sound of glass tinkling to the ground. We stood, relieved, as we looked on the tiled floor now covered in tiny blue coffins of ice.

"Well that was... interesting," Kasabian muttered while flicking ice encased bugs off of his shoulders.

Still tucked into a crouch, Ferrum lowered his arms, eyes peering up. "Are they gone?" he whispered. He jerked upright and cleared his throat after taking notice of Vashti who was doing her best to suppress a giggle.

"Still eager to enter first, Ferrum?" I teased.

His face reddened, almost matching his hair.

"Move aside, kid," Citadel scoffed, brushing past the young soldier and kicking the door open.

The room was indeed the source of the rancid smell, and I wondered if this was why Dumas had spent so much of his time in Pardus. Who could live with this rancid odor?

I entered after Citadel, Dryden staying outside in the hall. Even his strong instinct to protect me could not overcome the intolerable stench for him. Kasabian came in after me, a torch illuminating the room. Jewels were inlaid everywhere, from the bedposts to the hearth to the windowsill.

Tacky.

We combed through every inch and searched every side room, yet we could not find the source of the odor. I sighed, rubbing my temples. The smell was not helping my head, the pain seeming to increase by the hour.

Citadel strode over to where I leaned against a gilded desk. "Are you alright, Your Majesty?" he asked, brows furrowed and lips pursed.

I pressed the heel of my palm into my forehead, replying, "I don't know. Something feels... *off*. I don't know what it is, but my head is killing me and something inside of me senses a presence—something that unsettles my spirit."

"A presence?" he asked, eyebrows raised.

I shrugged, waving my hands in the air. "I don't know how to explain it."

Vashti had walked over while we had been talking. "I feel it too. Something... sinister."

Kasabian called out, "I don't know what you are talking about. The only thing I sense is my nostrils slowly decaying from this awful place."

Citadel rubbed the back of his neck as he answered, "I'm afraid I am not sure what you both mean. I can feel a certain heaviness to this place, but nothing particularly nefarious."

I wondered why Vashti and I felt uneasy while the others did not. Perhaps, there was a reason behind the difference in our perceptions. "I've never asked this before, but do you both believe in The Creator?"

"No, but I believe in you, my Queen," the Legate replied.

"I don't know," Kasabian answered, eyes downcast.

Then there was some weight to my theory, that only those with connections—those who believed—could sense the *un-rightness* of this place. Their belief in me would have to be enough for now, although I didn't know how they could overcome what we had to face, how their roles would be fulfilled in the prophecy without faith, but The Creator had called us together to this place for a reason.

Citadel leaned forward and whispered, "Your Majesty. You recognize this smell don't you? I was unsure at first, but once we entered these quarters, I became certain. This is the stench of corpses—"

"That's it. Someone else can be on dragon-sitting duty!" Raven Bone burst into the room, Sol dangling from his hand, her teeth sunk into the chief's palm.

I rushed over, prying the she-dragon's mouth from his flesh. Raven Bone brought his arm to his chest, blowing on the wound. I pulled Sol into me as she glared at him.

"What did you do?" I asked.

Raven Bone paused his blowing of air to reply, "Nothing. I just wanted to give her a little kiss on the snout."

I rolled my eyes and scoffed, "You're lucky she didn't tear your nose off."

Raven Bone shook his hand, the blood having already coagulated. "I liked the blue one better anyways," he told Sol.

"Where is Bahm?" I asked, but my question was answered as I scanned the room. Bahm slunk along the ground, legs darting forward and tongue flicking in and out. He stopped in front of a tapestry depicting a badger, the sigil of House Stallian. The he-dragon poked behind the cloth, a soft whining sound emitting from him.

As I walked over to investigate, Sol jumped from my arms and joined her brother. I yanked the tapestry to the side and gasped as a wooden door stared back at me. I went to open it, but Citadel rushed forward, knocking my hand away.

He positioned himself in front of me, brows drawn together and lips in firm creases. "I shall enter first, Your Majesty."

The Legate opened the door, and Kasabian handed him a torch, revealing a dark and damp staircase that led downwards

"Well everyone, let's go meet our destiny." It was my best attempt at an inspirational speech.

As he passed by me, Kas mumbled, "More like our deaths."

I flicked the back of his head, and he yelped, rubbing the spot with his hand as we continued to file in one by one, the path too narrow for even two people to stand shoulder to shoulder.

I called out to Dryden, *Are you coming or are you going to hide in the hall forever?*

A furry body crashed into the back of my thighs, causing me to stumble, but luckily I was able to catch myself on the rough wall. *Hey, careful!*

Dryden's ears flattened. *Sorry.*

I made sure Vashti was directly behind us, with Ferrum and a handful of guards bringing up the rear. The rest would stay in the castle and wait for Mordris and the rest of the men before joining us down in whatever pit we were headed into. The air was moist and musty, and water dripped down the walls the further we went.

"Slowing down!" Citadel hollered, "Never underestimate what water and stone can do to the grip of your shoes."

Eyes trained on the next step, I kept one hand on the wall as we descended.

CHAPTER FIFTEEN

LUX

My *stomach had ceased* growling, and I had given up attempting to keep track of the time that passed. It didn't matter anyways. No one was coming for me.

Was Valine okay? Was she safe? Had she already married another man? The Pirate King? Or the blind Chief? She had so many options, my beautiful bird. She was amazing. Too good for me. I hoped she was happy whoever she ended up with. Yes. It would be best if she forgot all about me. I was a worthless coward anyways.

I lay on the cold, damp cage floor, my body shivering uncontrollably and my teeth clattering to the point of pain. I wasn't sure why I shook with such violence. Perhaps it was the drop in temperature or perhaps my body was eating itself with no more fat to burn through.

Scraping against the stone alerted the arrival of the creature.

The poor little pup looks so pitiful.

The creature had long forsook talking aloud, seeming to relish that I was defenseless against its mental onslaughts. I banged my head against the floor, using what little strength I had in an attempt to banish its words. But it was futile, the thing's voice piercing my skull.

Your leopard cub is coming for you. Everything is working out splendidly.

What? Valine was coming for me? My heart leapt in my chest, and I smiled, the motion causing my already cracked lips to bleed. Wait. What did the creature mean about the latter? No. No. *No.*

I was the bait—a trap for her.

I tried to drag myself towards the bars, my bony fingers reaching towards the rusted metal rods, but my arm fell limply to the ground after a few seconds of exertion. I opened my mouth to cry out, to raise my voice in warning, but all that came out was an incoherent, raspy sound. I was too weakened by the extended lack of movement and nutrition, but there was still enough moisture within me for tears to come out as I mourned whatever terrible plan the creature had devised, distraught over my inability to protect my precious Little Bird.

The creature cackled and clapped around the cell, jubilant over its clever scheming.

I laid onto my back, the chill from the floor seeping into my bones. Was this how Valine's ice magic felt? Would she be able to use it?

I closed my eyes and prayed, *Please protect her. It's okay if I die, but she can't.*

The creature ceased its dance and yelped, scuttering away.

Suddenly, far across the room, a single fire in a giant bronze bowl illuminated twelve hooded figures. The flames were too far away to light my surroundings, but I could at least see the strange cloaked people who now raised their arms and began chanting.

It was a sharp and guttural sounding language, and I had never heard it before. Not that I was fluent in all the languages of Saego, but I could at least recognize them.

Their incantations became louder and echoed off the walls, which due to the firelight I could see were rough stones with water dripping and algae crawling along it. I was in some sort of cave. I did my best to study that which was visible, so that when Valine did rescue me I could relay the intel.

Unfortunately, the little that was illuminated was nothing of import, so I focused back on the figures. Their voices were a cacophony now, and did nothing to help my pounding head.

All of a sudden their heads jerked back causing their hoods to fall and reveal black hair and blue-ish white skin that looked as moist as the cavern walls. A strange gurgling overtook them, and one man stepped towards the woman to his right, and reaching beneath his cloak, he pulled out a rusted brown blade. He plunged it into the pale woman in front of him.

I gasped, the hair on my neck erect.

As her body slumped to the ground, the group's chanting softened to low hums, and the man with the knife knelt beside her and ripped her heart out, bones crunching and cracking and dark blue blood splattering everywhere. He lifted the still heart and said some words before tossing it into the fire. As it burned, moans of pleasure emitted from the remaining men and women, their fingers twitching and heads rolling back as they felt the effects of whatever ritual they had done.

The cascading light illuminated more of their faces and necks, dark vessels crawling like spider webs along their bodies. All those veins near the surface of their skin meant that they would be easier to make bleed.

A prayer escaped my lips, "Creator, please watch over her. Please keep her—"

My words were cut off as a scream pierced the air.

"It burns!" one of the cloaked men shouted as another woman shrieked and clutched her face.

The man who was still coated in blue blood whipped his head in my direction. He stalked towards me, head tilted in an unsettling position. He pointed a cobalt finger at me and hissed, "You! Stop those infernal prayers."

Ignoring his command—in fact all the more determined—I continued. "Give her victory over her enemies, and the strength to do what must be done."

More screams echoed in the cavern, bouncing off the walls and fueling my whispered pleas to the heavens. The man was almost to me now, one hand covering his ear, the other outstretched.

"Do not let her be overcome with rage or despair, but fill her with peace and joy. May your—"

My prayers were cut short as a sticky hand reached through the bars and gripped my neck.

A rotten stench blew into my face. "I told you to stop," the man growled. "As soon as she gets here, your purpose is no more. We couldn't harm her that day in the palace, but this is our domain. *He* cannot stop us now."

I clawed feebly at the fingers wrapped around my neck, desperate to breathe. *Help me!* I screamed in my mind, begging for Him to intervene.

The man yelped and released me, shaking his hand as if he had been burned as I collapsed to the floor.

Whatever comes, your will be done. I smiled through cracked lips as I laid on the floor, sending off one final prayer and savoring the sound of the men and women screeching.

CHAPTER SIXTEEN

VALINE

The stench was at its worst, and even our makeshift masks couldn't save our noses from the horrible onslaught. One poor soldier had even vomited, unable to bear the odor. Dryden grumbled and complained the whole way down while the dragons whined in a high pitch sound as they hobbled down. My ears and nose were both overwhelmed and with each step further into the dark abyss, the pain in my head increased. Vukan's pipe full of poppy didn't seem so repulsive now, and I yearned for something to ease the throbbing.

Kasabian coughed. "This is worse than when Amnys ate some bad squid and was blasting from his buttocks for days."

Some of the soldiers laughed as others did their best not to expel the contents of their stomach. I looked behind, pausing for a moment to check on Vashti. I was concerned that the pampered life the princess had lived would leave her unable to endure the current predicament. One hand was propped against the wall, the other covering her mouth and nose.

"How are you holding up?" I asked.

Her voice came out nasally as she pinched her nose. "Well it's definitely no rose bath."

I smiled beneath my mask, impressed with how well she adapted and handled everything thrown at her. But then the prophecy popped into my mind, and my lips turned down into a frown. There was still a sacrifice to be made. I would make sure it wasn't her, that Princess Vashti would live to see her eighteenth birthday, to get to see home again.

Down the staircase, the heads of the rest of my comrades bobbed as they descended. I closed my eyes, inhaled through my mouth, opened them, and exhaled. I began trudging down once more, my shoulders dragging by the weight of our endeavor.

With every step of our descent, the air got thicker, heavier, and felt almost suffocating. A dark presence permeated around us, and I worried what malevolent creature awaited us. No matter how powerful, no matter how vile, it would not stop me—would not keep me—from getting my husband back. Somehow, we would vanquish whatever it was. I refused to place such a burden upon my descendants. It would end with me, with us, one way or another, and I was determined that my friends and soldiers would leave this place alive. There would be no more Sokahs or Callars.

My feet were aching by the time we reached the end of the stairs, and I yearned to sit in a hot bath. After this I could rest, sleep as much as I desired. My hand went to the dagger on my hip, my fingers tracing the metal, soaking in its steady comfort. It was hard and cold, like my ice, and I finally understood that my ice magic may not be useful in peace time, but it could be the harbinger of it, ensure such an era had the ability to arise.

We walked for a few feet in a damp and cool corridor, our light diminished, the torches weakened by whatever dark entity resided here. We came upon a metal door, rusted from the water. Citadel reached for the handle, but as he pulled, it broke off, red and orange flakes falling to the ground.

"Oh, look who has big muscles," Kasabian teased, but Citadel glared at him return.

It didn't phase Kasabian though, who stood with a grin plastered on his face that was faintly visible beneath his mask, but I could see that it stopped at his mouth, that in his eyes was the serious reality of danger.

Citadel sucked in a breath and braced his arm as he slammed his body into the door. It burst open with ease, rusty powder floating in the air as it swung open with a groan. We entered the cavern, the torches hardly emitting any light, only a few steps in each direction visible.

"Walk slowly, weapons out," I commanded.

The sound of swords being unsheathed and crossbows being nocked echoed in the cave. I padded forward, Dryden on one side and the two dragons on the other.

A strange groan emitted from the shadows, and my skin turned cold, the hair on my arms standing upright. We turned towards the sound. Holding out my hand, I motioned for a torch, and as soon as I felt it in my palm, I swung my arm towards the source of the noise. My eyes strained in the dim light, the flames of my torch battling with the heavy darkness that was thicker than a moonless night.

An arched cage with rusted metal and strange symbols carved into the bars sat nestled in the rock wall, but inside was a shape—a woman.

She moved, her head creeping up in slow motion, and I gasped. The woman looked to be on death's doorstep, and as she opened her mouth, using what precious energy she had left, I nearly vomited at the sight of broken and missing teeth, the little I ate that morning attempting to expel itself. She reached out a withered and blood crusted hand. All the fingernails were missing.

"Have you come to end my suffering?" she asked in a raspy croak.

My chest tightened and my stomach twisted into knots as I replied with a voice filled with sorrow, "Yes, we will save you."

I called Vashti over, and she immediately set to work unlocking the cell. With a click, the lock released and clattered to the ground, and the woman crawled forward. Vashti and I gently pulled her to her feet as the woman whimpered. Holding her on each side, we walked towards the entrance where most of my men waited, but all of a sudden her head was ripped backwards, a screech escaping from her throat.

The jarring motion caused Vashti and I to stumble, releasing our grip on the woman. I whipped around and saw a cloaked man who had appeared out of nowhere holding her, his fingers curled around her scalp and a blade in his other hand.

The man hissed, "There is nothing more delightful than crushing hope, then snuffing out the little bit of light that keeps one going." Then he sliced open her throat.

"No!" I yelled, hand outstretched, shock slowing my reaction.

Citadel rushed forward, wrapped an arm around my waist and yanked me back, Vashti following on instinct. As we retreated, light suddenly enveloped the cavern, illuminating cloaked figures lining the perimeter with more cages scattered around the room. Some were empty, others had dark reddish brown markings painted on the floors—only visible because the inhabitants were now nothing but bone. On one side was what looked to be an elevated bowl, dried blood crusting its rim; I had no desire to imagine what it was used for.

On the opposite side of the cave, something else caught my eyes, and I sucked in a breath, my fists tightening. A name lodged in my throat as I moved forward.

Before I could take another step, someone appeared next to me, just like the last time in my court. Dryden snarled, the dragons emitted a high-pitched whistle, and my men stepped forward, blades pointed at him. I turned around, the hair raised on the back of my neck as my eyes met the familiar black teeth.

I sent a wave of ice to swallow him, but a wall of black mist crushed the ice into thousands of tiny crystals. Lifting a hand, I prepared to attack, but shadowy cords snaked around me, pinning my arms and feet.

"The cub is here," Noctis said in a sing-song voice, and a gust of his breath blew into my face, carrying the scent of decay as a dark blue tongue grazed his lips.

Dryden pounced, but before all his paws could even leave the ground, he was slammed back to the floor with a wave of shadows that looked just like Raven Bone's. I whipped my head back and forth looking for the Waodani Chief, but he was nowhere to be found. The rest of my men were all frozen in place, wisps of shadows pinning their legs and preventing them from coming to aid their queen.

Screeching pierced my ears, and I turned to where a cage was careening towards us, rusty metal scraping against the rocky floor as black clouds shoved it. Noctis grabbed the back of my neck, fingers digging into my skin, but I paid no heed, my eyes trained on one thing. One person.

Lux laid on the floor of the rusted cell, a husk of a human. His once luscious hair was dulled and thin, his skin sagged on his bony frame, and soft croaks emitted from cracked lips.

His glazed eyes peered up at me, a whisper escaping his throat. "A dream..."

A sob escaped my throat, and my heart felt like it was being ground between two stones like a flour mill. My arms instinctively attempted to reach out towards Lux, but the shadows bound me in place.

"Let me go!" I hissed through my teeth.

"Ah, ah, ah," Noctis tsked. "The wolf pup is payment, a blood debt."

I glared at the pale man. "What do you mean?"

Noctis explained, "Vukan bargained with us decades ago, but since he failed to uphold his end, the breach of contract came with a price." His gaze turned towards Lux whose dull eyes stared at us, his hand outstretched.

My mind raced trying to comprehend. A deal? Were all those atrocities the result of some contract? "So you made Vukan do all that? The overthrowing, the kidnapping, the wars?"

Noctis corrected, "Make no mistake, Vukan chose us, gave himself over to us. We cannot make someone do anything, rather we are always invited in." He paused, glancing around at the bone littered cages. "Well, sometimes we come knocking."

"Why did you help him take my throne but not help him keep it?"

"He promised an empire, but he couldn't even maintain a single kingdom. That pathetic excuse for a king was ambitious but without the means and skills to fulfill his desires. He was too weak, so we had to cut our losses. Now you, we would love to assist you. A young girl was able to defeat a *king*. That takes skill and fortitude. You are so clever and strong to have accomplished so much." His words came out coated in sugar, like a father praising their child's accomplishments. "We can give you power, more than you can imagine," he promised with honey dripping from each word like a sweet song.

A flash of white, and suddenly I found myself standing atop the Sanguis Mountains above Pardus, overlooking the city and forests, and the Xian river cut through the land to the left side of the capital. I felt as light as rays of sunshine, and I looked down, my feet not even making a dent in the dirt. My head whipped back to the man standing next to me. Noctis reflected the sunlight, appearing iridescent. He looked almost... beautiful.

Gentle hands guided my gaze back towards Racour. "I could ensure that no one is ever able to take this from you, that Racour will be safe and prosperous," he whispered with honey dripping from his words. His hands gently turned me around to face the border, where Racour, Eboc, and Manchur all conjoined. "I could even give you *all* of this. You would be an empress; you would rule all of Saego."

My heart began to gallop like a horse, my eyes widening. There would be peace in unity. I could make sure there was no fighting, that there would be no one to threaten the stability of the land.

The smell of almonds and flowers drifted into my nose, and a faint image of skin like dusk, eyes like chestnuts, and black vines of hair drifted in front of me. Eboc was Zasper's home.

I crushed my fingers into my palm and sucked in a breath. *No.* Such delusions were what Sebastien had thought. No, I could never be a conqueror; I would be a haven. I would lead the country I belonged to, and if others decided to join it, it would be of their own will.

Turning back to Noctis, I replied, "I don't need to be an empress."

His jaw clenched as his eyes narrowed for a fraction of a second before his lips parted in a crescent. "Very well," he said as he flicked his hand in the air.

Now we were in the gardens of the palace, but not as they currently were. Gone were the dull bushes and state of disarray, and in their stead were the roses and lilies, snapdragons and daisies, with the opal tree standing regally in the center. But there was a figure under its white blossom branches, a woman with long flowing hair, soft features, and paint still smeared across her purple dress.

"Mother—" my words caught in my throat, but my legs still functioned, flinging me towards the woman under the tree.

I collapsed to the ground in front of her, my hands grasping at her skirts as I peered up into the woman who had bore me, who had abandoned me in this world.

"I miss you," I choked out, my eyes watering.

She looked down, smiling, as she reached out a soft hand and placed it against my cheek. I leaned into it. I could almost feel the warmth of her smooth, callous-free skin. She had never bothered to train in weaponry, but I no longer cared, no longer judged her for it. I just wanted my mother.

Her melodic voice carried in the air like a songbird's as she spoke, "My little warrior princess. Are you still picking fights, trying to be valiant?"

Smiling squished my eyes together as I sniffled. "You know I've always wanted to be a hero."

Her other hand began stroking my hair as she asked, "And are you one?"

My face dragged down by the anticipation of disappointment as I whispered, "No. I am no one special."

"Correct."

I jerked my head up, mouth agape. "What?"

My mother's soft features turned hard, her brows pointed down and her lips curled in disgust. Her voice came out accusatory, stinging like a hundred needles. "If you had been someone truly heroic, then you wouldn't have let me die!" Her hands that had been comforting me seconds ago now clamped around my neck, red rage burning in her eyes and spittle flying from her mouth as she yelled, "Why didn't you save me?"

The pressure on my neck made speaking difficult, and I wheezed the words out, "I'm sorry. I—"

Her face was in front of mine, full of revulsion. "All that magic and royal blood is wasted on someone like you!"

"Mother, I—"

My words were cut off as a whisper slithered into my ear, "I could give you more power, more magic, so that you will never lose someone you love again, never fail to protect your loved ones and citizens. You'll be able to kill your enemies with just a thought."

My mother's hands wrapped around my neck preventing me from looking at Noctis, but I felt him. No amount of floral scents would be able to mask his rotten breath.

As I stared up at the eyes of my mother—no, this was not my mother. My mother had only turned to violence one time in her life. *To save me.* The raging woman in front of me was a figment, some manipulation of reality created by *him.*

"N-no," I choked out, my lungs beginning to burn from the lack of air.

Noctis growled, and from the corner of my eye I saw his hand flash.

We were back in the cage filled cavern, but no one else was moving or speaking. My comrades' faces were frozen, almost like statues. Another illusion then.

He crouched down, blue tinted fingers stretching out towards Lux. Noctis shoved aside Lux's hair to better reveal his face, and my heart felt like it was being crushed in a stampede of hooves. My poor Lux. Blood crusted his lips, his skin was dull, and his eyes were as lifeless as charcoal.

Noctis crowed, "If you pledge yourself to us, if you give yourself to me, then I will allow him to live, and no harm shall befall him."

Silence.

I was probably a terrible person for not rejecting it right away, but as I stared at my husband, I felt inclined to accept. He who had no one to fight for him almost all his life, I could finally protect him—save him. I fell to my knees and crawled forward.

I knew he couldn't hear me, but as I traced his face with my finger, I whispered, "I love you."

I could see Noctis grinning, could see the gloating in his eyes at his apparent victory.

Pressing my two fingers to my lips, I reached through the bars to place it on Lux's forehead. Then I stood and turned towards Noctis.

"I'll save him or die trying, but if I do free him, it will not be due to a deal made with you," I hissed.

A dark shadow casted over his face as he snarled, "Fine."

He gestured with his hand once more, and I felt my feet press firm against the ground. The growling of Dryden and the murmurs of confusion and fear amongst my men signaled we were back to reality, the black wisps once more binding me in place.

"A shame. You would have been so much more fun on our side," he chided. Noctis smiled, but it was a wicked and sadistic expression, fingers wiggling in delight. "Now that you have refused, we shall begin."

I tried my best to sound strong, to ignore the fearful dread sprouting in my stomach. "Begin what?"

Noctis grinned. "The process of breaking you. I wanted to kill you actually, but *He* said I couldn't."

I glared. "Who?"

Noctis's nose flared. "I believe you call Him, *The Creator*." He spat the last word out, as if it was poison in his mouth. "He granted us permission to hurt you, to torture you, to bring your life to ruins, but He said we couldn't kill you. Really, I don't understand how you could trust such a cruel deity. He even hid your magic from us, so we couldn't take it. Oh and that little prophet. Good thing that old man is dead now. Pesky thing. That Egann was always getting in the way."

Through gritted teeth I seethed, "How dare you? I will destroy you!" My body fought uselessly against the magic bonds that held me down, and I resembled a flopping fish more than anything intimidating.

Noctis clapped his hands with a sickening pleasure. "No, no. That is our job," he sung and pointed to my right, and my eyes followed the direction of his finger.

Without so much as a sound, one of the Fallen grabbed one of my comrades nearest to her and sunk her teeth into his neck. I shouted, but it did no good as flesh tore and blood sprayed as the cloak-clad woman ripped his throat out. She let the man's body fall to the floor in an oozing heap, but my eyes paid no mind to the dead man as I was unable to move my gaze away from the veins that wriggled and protruded from pale skin. My stomach twisted as the woman's eyes blazed with sadistic euphoria, fingers twitching at the influx of power.

Another one of the Fallen caught one of my soldiers staring at his gold spikes that protruded from his gums. "Oh, do you like them?" the Fallen member asked. "It is part of our initiation ritual. Removing an aspect of yourself to make way for something better." The man smiled and ran his tongue over his gilded fangs.

The soldier trembled in the man's grip as shadow magic kept the poor soldier's arms pinned to his side, unable to defend himself. The Fallen inhaled, as if relishing the scent of fear. Then he ripped the soldier's neck open with his teeth, scarlet showering the Fallen's face.

I cursed, tears welling in my eyes as rage boiled in my stomach. I hated them—wanted them all dead.

They all turned their attention to us, wicked smiles dancing on their faces and eyes full of malicious excitement.

Shadow hands gripped my chin and forced me to look at their leader. "Have you been enjoying our gift?" Noctis asked while gesturing to his head.

My eyes widened as understanding flashed through me. The headaches had started from that day he came to court and had been getting worse ever since, and they were all because of him. I wondered if all those nightmares were caused by him too. However, I couldn't be sure since I had suffered from nightmares for a long time. I wasn't sure which terrible things in my existence were influenced by him or what was simply life's cruelty.

A voice scraped inside my head. *That was just a taste of what I am capable of. I will relish seeing you scream.*

And scream I did.

CHAPTER SEVENTEEN

VALINE

The pain was unbearable, as if all my bones were breaking simultaneously and lightning had struck my body, causing burns on my skin and my limbs to tremble like an earthquake. I managed to look down, expecting to see blood and scalded flesh, but everything looked normal. My teeth were glued to each other as searing agony blazed through my body. I writhed as it swept through, thousands of needles stabbing me and a strong grip causing my heart to explode from the pressure. I attempted to gather my bearings, to strategize, but the pain made it impossible as my vision clouded.

No matter how badly it hurt, I wouldn't die. *Couldn't* die.

Cackling and screams echoed in the cavern as we were all tormented by the Fallen.

Then it all stopped.

It could have lasted seconds or years; I had no way of knowing except as I shook my head, my jaw still clenched, I looked up to see my men flooding through the entrance we had come through. It must have been mere minutes despite feeling like an eternity. Our masks had fallen away from the writhing, but the stench of death was replaced with the metallic tang that emitted from the bodies of my killed comrades. I'd make them pay for each one.

I sighed in relief as Mordris and Falchor burst into the cavern, ranks of soldiers trailing behind them. But someone unexpected was with them: Zasper. Her hair was braided back and leather armor strapped to her body with a dark wood staff in her hand. I didn't know how she found us, whether she had decided to come along with Mordris, but the how didn't matter. She was here; she came. She came not for a prophecy, not for her own ideas of what was best for me and Racour, she came for *me*. They had come just in time to—

A blast of darkness flung towards them, some being knocked to the ground as others were thrown against the walls. Their heads cracked with a sickening thud. While I had been watching them enter, Noctis had slit one of my men's throats, crimson blood coating his hands, nostrils flaring as the power of the sacrifice infused into his body, his magic invigorated. His eyes were wide in delight as his black teeth dripped with red.

My ice roared in my veins, banging against my skin, begging to wreak havoc on the Fallen, but it could not fully emerge, something strong and heavy keeping it caged inside. I gritted my teeth, hatred as deep as the ocean filling my chest as I stared at the body of one of my soldiers.

A pale figure stepped into the cavern, deftly avoiding the grumbling bodies of my soldiers on the floor. When all this was over, I would scold him for arriving so late. Raven Bone reached up and pulled on the cloth that covered his eyes, and it floated to the ground. He was always so dramatic. Was even this a game to him? The Waodani chief smiled as shadowed swords formed in his hands.

Raven Bone twirled his twin blades of night. "I can't believe the apprentice is still alive," he scoffed, head tilted with his ear in the direction of his opponent.

Noctis' nostril flared and his eyes widened. "You're *her* offspring," he spat.

Small shadows pranced around Raven Bone's feet, but I couldn't tell whose magic it was. He replied with a grin on his face, "Still jealous of my mother? I see even centuries later you are still bitter about losing the chiefdom to her."

Panting from the pain, my mind tried to connect the dots. How could he possibly identify Noctis without seeing him? And his mother... I ground my teeth together, promising myself to rip into Raven Bone about his omission of who his mother was after all this was over.

Noctis hissed, and a dark figure swelled up behind him, like a monstrous shadow coming to life. "And yet she has long passed while I am still alive, more powerful than she ever was."

Raven Bone twisted his wrists, blades spinning. "Well, I think it's time to send you to your own afterlife, although it won't be so pleasant of a place as where my mother resides."

Noctis' lips upturned and his tongue ran over his teeth. "I will tear out your neck. Then you can meet your mother and He who scorned me." Noctis shouted, "Bring them out!"

A creaking sound emitted from a dark alcove, and two of the Fallen appeared, multiple chains clasped in each hand. On the other end of those metal leashes were creatures that looked like perverted and tortured versions of the hounds used by hunters, no fur, no softness, only bare skin that looked burnt and eyes that glowed an unnatural bright yellow. Their teeth matched that of the Fallen, grotesque dark shards that were ready to slice us to pieces.

Raven Bone laughed, as he so often did in the face of a good fight. "Puppies! I can play that game, too."

He flicked his wrist and shadows sprung to life around him, taking form into great black beasts of darkness. The shadow wolves looked almost tangible, and I knew by the glint in Raven Bone's eyes that their snapping jaws would have a very real effect, which I was grateful I wouldn't have to experience for myself.

The mutilated mutts however, looked very ready to show me what they could do, drool and spittle flying as they snapped at the air, waiting for the command to be given to devour.

Whatever dark magic was involved with their killing, it was more powerful than anything I had experienced, granted that wasn't much. My arms and legs were still incapacitated, and while the two pale men were confronting each other, I looked around. Those of us who had first arrived were still pinned in place, black cords keeping us trapped while those who had just entered were still picking themselves up with groans and whimpers.

Vashti's face was filled with fear, and Kasabian was squirming, all the while his panicked eyes trained on the Percian Princess. I would have to trust that when we finally figured out how to get out of this situation, that he would take good care of her. I wouldn't be able to protect her once the real fighting started. Mordris rushed over to Ferrum, trying to yank him free of his constraints but to no avail. Zasper quickly regained her bearings and helped Falchor get to his feet. I made eye-contact with Citadel, his face a mixture of frustration and worry, his gaze dancing between me and Lux.

Movement towards Lux's cage caught my attention, but I was unable to do anything as I watched one of the Fallen approach him, his blue tongue running over sapphire teeth, a sense of helplessness cascading through me. The man yanked Lux's hand out and between the bars, and he stared at me as he cut his hand open, nostrils flaring as the scent of blood filled his nostrils and sparks danced in his eyes after hearing Lux cry out in pain.

My body didn't blaze with a fiery fury. Instead my bones chilled, a calm icy rage taking hold of me as my eyes glazed over with a hard resolution. *Help me save him!* I shouted to The Creator, and I felt my feet shuffle and my arms swinging loose.

The Fallen man shifted, prepared to make another cut on Lux's body, seemingly unaware of me freeing from the shadowy bonds.

Just as he was bringing his hand down, I lurched forward and seethed, "Don't touch my husband."

Ice exploded from the inside out of the Fallen man, blood spraying and body parts flying into the walls with a wet smack.

Growls and gasps emanated from around me, but all I could focus on was Lux, on the blood seeping from the wound where the Fallen had cut his palm, his hand hanging limply out of the cage. I wanted to burst the metal bars with my magic, but whatever engravings were on them were likely what had caused Lux to be unable to use his own, and I couldn't afford to waste my energy.

I whipped my head around to the rest of my comrades, my heart plummeting to my stomach as I steeled myself to see most of them deceased, but what I had thought had taken minutes had only been seconds. Relief washed over me seeing that no others had been killed.

Yet.

The rest of the Fallen were creeping towards my shadow-bound friends, and how I had broken free finally clicked.

"You have to pray to keep the voices out!" I shouted.

Whether they believed in Him or not, He believed in us, and He would be faithful to hear, no matter how small our own faith was. A symphony of prayers could be heard, some whispers, others bellowing, and suddenly we could move again, could silence the voices taunting us in our heads.

The Fallen hissed and screeched in a collective cry, clutching their heads as our prayers flew up, but it also caused the two holding the pack of hounds to drop their chains. The rabid dogs charged us, jaws snapping. My comrades all drew their weapons and prepared to fight, prayers never far from our lips as we worked to keep the black magic at bay.

I threw up a wall of ice to stop the mutts, so that we could focus on the cloaked men and women first. The beasts threw themselves against the murky blue shield, and with each hit the cracks in the barrier grew larger. It wouldn't last long, so we had to act with haste and get rid of as many of the Fallen as we could before the dogs inevitably broke through.

A yelp echoed on the other side of the barrier as Raven Bone's shadow wolves collided with the Fallen's hounds, squealing and snarling mixing into one. But there were more hounds than wolves, and the ones not entangled with Raven Bone's creations were still clawing at the ice wall. There were also a multitude of Fallen on this side of the barrier, and despite the prayers, they were slowly creeping their way towards us.

A prayer that Egann used to say popped into my mind, calming the panicked seas roaring inside me.

Oh mighty Creator, who watches us from above. I unsheathed my blade.

Praise be to you who is able. I jogged towards the nearest Fallen who was covering their ears.

May I obey your commands and carry your words wherever I go. I stabbed her in the stomach, and after wrenching my weapon from her torso, I swung my sword at her neck just for good measure.

Provide for me. I turned to the next one.

Forgive our offenses, and help us forgive those who commit offenses against us. Blue blood began to coat the cavern floor, making it slick and the air smell even more rancid.

Lead according to your glory, and aid us in times of struggle. This time a hound who had broken through came at me, seeming to be unaffected by the prayers, and I readied my blade.

We thank you for hearing our prayers. My sword protruded from its head, its heavy body dragging my arms down with it as it slammed into the ground, lifeless.

A fist slammed into my face, and I reeled backwards, my sword getting left behind where it was stuck inside the mutt. My hand automatically clutched my throbbing and stinging face.

A Fallen man, blue vein bulging from his forehead, hissed through ruby fangs, "I will relish drinking your blood. Magic makes it taste even better, and drinking it means I get all the power it has to offer, courtesy of the Dark One."

His eyes glanced towards Lux, and rage stormed inside me. I could picture it in my head, the Fallen taunting him—torturing him—as they cut him. How dare he drink my husband's blood. I would make sure the man's own coated the floor he stood on. My lips curled into a feral crescent, crimson creeping between my teeth and scarlet slithering down my chin.

I spat, red saliva landing at the cloaked man's feet. He snarled, a wild and animalistic sound, and charged me, a black blade in his hand. Grabbing the dagger from my waistband, I shifted all my weight to my right leg, positioning it behind me as he drew closer. Despite the distance between me and his knife closing, I forced myself to wait, calming my rapidly beating heart. One second. Two seconds. Now.

Lunging, I slid under his right side and sliced his heel with my dagger, severing his tendons. I whipped around, and he stumbled to the floor, blue gushing from his leg. As much as some sinister part of me wished to prolong his suffering, to cut him slowly, tearing his flesh until his body gave out, I knew that was not right, nor wise given there were hounds and Fallen who were still trying to kill me. I shoved that sadistic thought far down inside and swiped at his neck, a blue line forming across his throat as his body crumpled.

I heard a snarl from behind me and turned just in time to see the wide and dripping jaws of a hound. I flung up a hand, and ice encased its snout. Crashing into the floor by the unexpected weight, I spun and plunged my blade into the base of its skull, all movement ceasing. But another mutt was launching towards me, and I steeled myself to feel the searing pain of its jaws sinking into my flesh. A flash of gray barreled into it as Dryden sank his fangs into the creature's neck.

You're getting sloppy, Dryden scolded.

A half-smile tugged at my lips as I fought to catch my breath. *That's what you're for.*

I took a moment to glance at where Raven Bone and Noctis had been standing, my icy barrier shattered and almost nonexistent. They'd disappeared in a black cloud, hisses of pain and shouts of frustration emitting from the darkness.

After what could have been seconds or minutes, a pale body was thrown across the room, and the dark cloud vanished. Noctis grinned, eyes ablaze with triumph as the

Waodani chief lay prostrate on the ground. My mouth hung open at the sight of them.

Raven Bone had more magic than anyone I was aware of, and he was a skilled fighter. I knew that when we had the conclave he had taken it easy on me—hadn't been trying to kill me. Yet even he was not able to defeat Noctis, and my stomach knotted in despair. How were we supposed to defeat them?

But Raven Bone wasn't a part of the prophecy. I wasn't sure what the sacrifice part meant, if that meant all of us would have to die, if our combined lives would end this great abomination, or if just one of us had to be a sacrifice. I looked around at those who were written on the scroll. As I'd been fighting, I had ended up a good distance away from the cage, but Vashti and Kasabian were standing guard over Lux. Sol's back arched like an angry cat, sharp teeth bared in a warning. Zasper was there too with her staff twirling in her hand.

Kasabian shouted over the cacophony of fighting, "If something happens to you, Naghmeh will kill me."

Vashti was working on getting the cell open, her hands shaking as she tried to pick the lock with a hairpin. "This is nothing compared to Naghmeh's anger, so I suggest you try your hardest to protect me!"

Citadel was locked in combat, sword slashing at one of the Fallen and doing his best to avoid the hounds. Falchor's sword protruded from another Fallen's head, and he yanked his weapon free just in time to block a second cloaked figure's blade. Ferrum and Mordris fought side by side dealing with three mutts. Dryden ripped out another hound's throat, his fangs coated in dark blood.

I turned my attention back towards Noctis, whose own eyes were locked on me.

From out of nowhere, Bahm darted towards Noctis, rows of teeth snapping and digging into his leg. Reaching down with a veiny hand, Noctis grabbed Bahm and ripped the dragon from his leg, a bluish blood oozing out. Noctis threw the dragon to the floor, a squeal erupting from him as he crashed with the ground. Dryden snarled and leapt to stand over the blue body on the floor, ignoring his own wounds that dripped blood onto the floor.

Without having to say a word, we attacked in tandem, my blade striking as Dryden's claws swiped at Noctis, blue and red blood mixing to create a dark purple that splattered like paint across the cavern. I willed for ice to encase Noctis' legs, but shadows seemed to guard his body in a protective barrier, demolishing the ice into tiny pieces. And no matter how many times our blows landed true, he still stood, black teeth revealed in a sneer. Noctis clamped his hand into a fist, and my head exploded into pain. I backed away, clutching the sides of my head, stumbling blindly. Falling to the floor and gasping for breath, I prayed, *Please help me!*

The pain ebbed, and my vision cleared in time to see Dryden flung backwards. Noctis stalked towards the leopard, but a flash of blue darted towards his legs again. Bahm, the normally pale blue fur along his spine stained dark, sunk his teeth once more in Noctis' calf. In return, he wrapped his fingers around the small dragon, pulled him off and brought him to his own mouth and bit into his leg. Blood exploded everywhere as Noctis tore the dragon's leg off—eliciting a squeal of terror and pain from Bahm—before discarding the creature, tossing him to the ground.

Dryden shook his head and drug himself towards the heap of cobalt scales, a whimper escaping the proud cat's throat as he nuzzled the unmoving body. His nose pushed the dragon. Nothing. A snarl erupted from him, full of rage and indignation at the tiny form on the ground. Dryden stood, flanks rising up and down in rapid succession despite all the crimson soaked fur and gashes that seeped blood into his face. I knew that as his claws un-sheathed—some oozing scarlet from where they had been torn out—that he would kill the man who had hurt Bahm. Or he would die trying.

I stood again and charged towards Noctis, a dagger resting firmly in my palm. Every few seconds between slashes and punches, I sent up a prayer to render the dark magic useless. I faked a swipe to his neck before wrenching my arm down towards his abdomen while simultaneously sending an ice shard towards his back, but it was futile. Noctis blasted a wave of shadows at me, causing me to crash to the ground, my blade clattering to a halt a few steps away from where I lay sprawled on the floor. The ice shard clattered to the ground behind him.

Noctis pulled out his own blade, a rusted thing that looked like it would create a nasty infection with the smallest prick. Exhaustion weighed me down, and he towered over me as I fought to catch my breath. He careened down, knife ready to puncture my heart. I whipped my arms up, using all my strength to hold him back which was made all the more difficult due to gravity. The blade had been a breath away from impaling me. I sent ice to encase his head, but black shadows crushed all my ice into dust. I wasn't sure how much I had left in me before my well ran dry.

A ball of frustration formed in my chest. What was the point of The Creator giving me magic if it would end up being so useless? Noctis had every advantage over me: strength, magic, position. I wouldn't be able to keep the blade at bay forever. An idea sparked in my mind.

I was going to hate this. I was going to hate this so very badly. But directing the stab was a lot easier than holding him back, and at least I would get the knife out of his hands.

My arms trembled from the strain of keeping him away, but I dredged up what strength I had and shoved the blade towards the right side of my chest. Having used my last bit of strength, my arms gave out as the blade plunged into me just above my breast creating an inferno of pain that blazed through my right arm and torso. I gritted my teeth, taking the opportunity to shove my palm up Noctis' nose, emitting a satisfying crunch. He reeled back clutching his face, and I crawled backwards. I managed to get to my knees, and I prayed that I wouldn't bleed to death as I yanked the knife out of my flesh.

The blade was coated in crimson, and my jaw clenched as my grip tightened. Dizziness overtook me, and I swayed. Perhaps my gamble hadn't been worth it. Noctis was down for the moment, but I could see our numbers dwindling, screams ringing as men were torn apart by the mutts or shredded by the Fallen's gem fangs.

Death had come, come for us all, and I didn't know how to stop it.

We are losing. Have you brought us all here just to perish? My nose stung and my body trembled as I pleaded—no—yelled at The Creator. I propped myself up against the wall and steadied my uneven breathing. *Take me, but don't let them suffer. I'll do anything, but please, just don't abandon us now.*

I scanned the cavern, my eyes landing on the cage where my closest friends were standing, where Zasper was. As I watched, my chest warmed, seeing her defend Lux, hold back the hordes and hounds with her staff, watched as one of the hounds bit into her calf. She gritted her teeth, grunting as she brought her staff down onto the creature's head with a sickening crack. As a leopardess defends her cubs, so did Zasper defend my husband, guarding what was precious to me, but she was precious to me as well.

I would give anything to keep them safe, to end this battle. I knew everything was happening in seconds, but as I realized what could be done, what had to be done, to end this, to save them, everything slowed. The gushing blood, the vicious snarls, the cracking of bones, the bodies falling to the ground, and the screams of pain and terror. One breath, two breaths.

Noctis was the strongest, the foe of old. If he was gone, they'd have a chance of killing the rest.

I love you and Lux and Zasper. Tell them for me somehow, Dryden.

I heard his voice in my head, and it was the angriest it had ever sounded, even more than when I had pinched his ears. *Valine! What are you doing? You said until the end!*

Ignoring him, I exhaled, conjuring what little magic remained and charged. I flung myself at Noctis, shock flashing in his eyes as his nostrils flared, and wrapped my body around his, my arms pinning his own to his side. We fell to the floor, and I willed my ice to carry out my bidding.

Freezing cold enveloped us.

Then there was nothing.

LUX

Although my vision was hazy and my head pounded, I was able to think clearly now that that *thing* was out of my head. Warm hands wrapped underneath me and carried me out of the cell. My head lolled back, and I saw the wavy dark hair and hooked nose.

"Hello, pirate," I managed to croak out.

A half smile that didn't distract from the sadness in his eyes formed on his face. "Your Highness, you've looked better."

If I'd had the strength to laugh, I would have.

The cold, hard cavern wall met my back as Kasabian laid me down, the smell of the wet stone masked by the scent of death. In front of me, a battle was still waging. Green scales darted towards me as Sol collided with my chest, eliciting a wheeze. My arm shaking, I patted her back, her fur soft against my palm.

Kas looked back at us. "Take good care of him, you weird looking lizard," he said before taking off back into the fray of the battle. Sol whistled sharp and high, and if she wasn't so worried about me she would have tried to take a chunk out of the pirate-turned-king's calf.

My eyes scanned the room.

Citadel was locked in duel with one of the cloaked men, emerald teeth tinged with scarlet blood. I lifted up a prayer for my loyal guard as I could do nothing but watch in horror. Raven Bone rode atop a strange looking dog, holding a shadowy rope that wrapped around the creature's neck as it snapped at the chief. Zasper was nearby, attending to a wounded soldier as another stood watch, blade drawn and dripping.

To my far left was Mordris, his age not slowing his arm as he swung his weapon, fighting back to back with his nephew. One of the cloaked figures launched themselves at Ferrum, who was too preoccupied with a mutt to notice, but Mordris did. I tried to call out a warning to Ferrum, but it was too late. Mordris flung himself in between his nephew and the Fallen. The sickening squelch of flesh echoed in the cavern as two blades met their mark: one through Mordris' chest and the other protruding from the body of the Fallen. They slumped to the ground as Ferrum cut down the hound, turning to crouch and cradle his uncle.

I was just close enough to hear but too far to help.

"Tell your brother I'm proud. Tell your mother I'm sorry. I love you all." Each word pumped out blood from his wound, and all too soon, movement ceased.

Ferrum had no time to mourn as another man with silver teeth lunged towards them.

I cursed, loathing my inability to aid them. My heart thundered in my chest, my eyes wide as I realized I hadn't seen Valine. There. At the far side of the cavern was my wife and her leopard. But what was beneath Dryden? That dark blue hump—*no*.

My body somehow found the moisture to create tears as I searched for any signs of life. He was too still. There was too much blood.

Dryden stood over him, his lips curled back in a snarl. Noctis was close by, and so was Valine, their gazes pinned to each other. My heart skipped a beat at the sight of her.

She started sprinting towards him, but there was no blade in her hand. What was she doing? I couldn't see Noctis' face as she collided with him, as gray ice erupted and engulfed them. I reached out, my mind screaming but my words only came out in a hoarse whisper, "Valine!"

CHAPTER EIGHTEEN

Lux

It had been three months since the Fallen had been defeated, since Valine, my wife, my queen, had ceased to breathe. After she had taken out Noctis, the rest of the Fallen weakened, seeming to become less powerful after he was dead. The hounds had also collapsed where they stood, whatever life they possessed had been connected to his, or rather his dark magic. It was only a few more minutes before they were all disposed of. Unfortunately, the cost was far too high, too many had paid with their lives, half the soldiers who had come to rescue me dying in the process. Like my Little Bird.

The sun shone through the window, reflecting off the ice covered form of High Queen of Racour. Beneath the murky blue, blood still coated her body, and her arms were still in the shape of an embrace—eerily statuesque. The giant tomb of ice that had encased both her and Noctis had cracked in half of its own accord—a mercy from The Creator. We sent Noctis to the bottom of the ocean in his icy coffin, sinking into a watery abyss.

However, the rest of it could not be broken, no matter how many picks and hammers were used, the tools all shattered before the ice did.

I sat down on the cushioned chair in front of her, Bahm and Sol scampering in behind me as they often did, albeit the cobalt dragon was slower as he was still getting used to three legs. Bahm curled into a ball under my chair, while Sol climbed her way to the top of the ice mound, taking up her guard post, the sunlight shining through the fur along her spine like a green flame.

"Princess Vashti sent for Ferrum, inviting him to visit Percia as a royal guest," I explained, fingers grazing the ice. "She also said that her father is no longer upset with her for leaving against his wishes. As I told you before, he was irate at her for disobeying him, for putting herself in such danger, but with time and many discussions, I think they came to an understanding."

I chuckled without much enthusiasm. "He actually almost did try to go to war with Racour, but the queen talked him down. It seems that her faith in her daughter and in The Creator might be stronger. But I understand him," I paused, eyes drilling through the icy barrier that kept us apart, "wanting to protect those you love, even if it isn't in line with The Creator's plan."

I traced the outline of her face, so calm—resigned to its fate. "Princess Zasper returned home now that the other rulers have agreed on my regency. Oh right, we picked a replacement for House Stallian. Queen Laika of House Aryll. I think you would approve of the choice." I sighed, my hand dropping to my lap.

My chin quivered, and my eyes blurred. "You promised you would never leave me," I whispered, my voice cracking. "But don't worry. I'll forgive you. Just come back to me, Val."

I sniffled and wiped the tears away as I heard someone approaching. Citadel strode into the room, long legs cutting through the distance, and fell to his knees in front of me. He had suffered some serious injuries in the battle and had only recently been released from the healer's ward; it was his first time seeing the queen. I had visited him a few times once I had recovered enough strength to do so, but during most of those, he had been too incoherent from the pain tonics.

He bowed, his head kissing the stone floor. "Forgive me, Your Highness. Your command was to protect Her Majesty, and I failed. I am unworthy of my position."

I had never heard him sound so broken, so sorrowful. He was always a serious yet strong fellow, always resolute in his quiet confidence, and I had been amazed that we got along so well despite our opposite personalities. I knew that his greatest strength of loyalty would also bring him great guilt.

I leaned forward and grabbed his shoulders. "You have served me well as my personal guard for years, and you will continue to serve Her Majesty as well. She will come back to us."

He peered up at me, the faintest ember of hope sparking in his eyes. "I will not fail you again."

I shook my head and pulled him up. "You have never once failed me."

At first my body froze in shock as Citadel embraced me, the first time he had ever done so, but after a moment I relaxed, wrapping my arms around him.

"I love you, brother," I muttered. He was a better family than those who I'd shared blood with, who had worried about me when my father decided to "teach me" a lesson—which tended to involve a cane to the calves or blade to the back. He or Rosalva were always the ones to nurse my wounds.

"My brother..." he whispered.

As we pulled apart, I told him, "I've never once regretted picking you as my personal guard, never once had anything other than complete trust in you. As far as Her Majesty is concerned, she knew what she was doing and not even a mountain could block her way when she made up her mind."

Citadel nodded, eyes drifting towards Valine. "I will leave you be then. If you need me, I'll be outside." He turned to the block of ice and saluted to his sovereign before exiting the room and leaving us alone.

Placing my hands on the giant block of ice, I conjured my fire until the area beneath my hands glowed like embers. Everyday for the past three months, even in my emaciated state in which I had to be carried into the room, I came and infused my magic until my well was empty. There was barely a dent in it even after all that time.

Whenever I wasn't there, Dryden was, protecting his companion even in her current state. He would go out to hunt and return, tail drooping and head hanging low. If anyone other than myself or the dragons came near, he would growl with the threat of being torn to shreds.

I vowed to continue my daily ritual, even if I was gray and wrinkled by the time it all melted. The well of magic ebbing, I gasped for breath as my arms trembled, and I leaned my forehead against the cold barrier.

"I'm on the shore."

A *few weeks later*, I entered the room as I did everyday, Dryden absent for one of his hunting excursions, but a shout escaped my lips. The ice had cracked into two, the halves lying prostrate on the floor, but there was no body, no Valine. I rushed towards it, my knees barking as they collided with the ground. She had been there just last night when I had come to say goodnight.

"I'll be careful the next time I ask The Creator for a long rest."

My body froze, my limbs locking together. I turned slowly, carefully, not wanting to wake from whatever dream this was, as if it could be spooked like a scared horse, not wanting to be disappointed when there would be inevitable emptiness, the voice a figment of my imagination and desire.

But when I turned, there she was, standing, *breathing*. I opened my mouth to speak, but nothing came out.

My Little Bird.

Valine smiled, and it was the most beautiful, most magical, most wonderful thing I had ever seen, more brilliant than the sun. I soaked it in like the earth soaks up the rain after a drought.

I whispered, my voice shaking, "You came back to me."

Her eyes watered as she replied, "I always keep my promises."

She walked forward and collapsed in front of me. Our arms wrapped around each other, and I shoved my face into her hair. It smelt terrible, and yet nothing could pry me from it. I inhaled, relishing the smell because it meant she was *alive*. She was cold to the touch, and I brought forth the slightest bit of magic and sent it into her.

My tears soaked her hair, and sobs racked my chest. I could hear her cries and sniffles as we held each other, unwilling to let go. I never wanted to let her out of my sight again.

I pulled back with reluctance, tracing her face with my eyes, engraving it in my mind lest she suddenly be taken away from me again.

Her eyes shimmered, and she smiled as she said, "I love you, Lux."

"You don't really mean that. You're just still out of it from the long sleep," I joked, afraid to take her words to heart as some disbelief that someone so amazing could love me was still present in the back of my mind. The handsome pirate with a silky smirk appeared in my head.

But she shook her head, hands cupping my cheeks. "All that time ago, Vukan thought he was chaining me by marrying me to his son, but he had done just the opposite. Our relationship is the source of freedom that comes with hope, of not being alone in the dark. I would slay any monster in that darkness to get you back, my husband, my friend, my hope. You. I choose you, Lux. I didn't choose our marriage, but I chose to stay. I love you, and I've been waiting to say those words for a long time."

I felt like I would burst into a thousand flames as my heart leapt in my chest. Before I could say or do anything, her face careened into mine, our lips crashing into each other in a long awaited meeting. In what felt like forever and not time at all, we pulled away, and my cheeks aching from how hard I was smiling.

"I love you, Valine, with my very life and being, I love you."

A strange sound, something between a whimper and a roar, emitted behind me. I turned my head, Dryden standing in the doorway, flanks panting. He must have felt it—Valine's heart—and ran back here.

A gray flash darted in front of me as Dryden barreled into Valine. I couldn't hear what the two said to each other, but whatever it was caused her to break out into tears again as she wrapped her arms around her companion. The ice leopard also appeared to cry, a strange whimpering coming from him.

She was considerate enough to include me in their conversation. "He said he felt it as soon as I came out, and he raced back from the forest. He also said that if I ever did something like that again, he would kill me himself."

I chuckled. "I admit, I share the sentiment."

After we soaked in each other's presence and thanked The Creator for this miracle, I called for the guards and instructed them to inform everyone that the queen was alive.

While we waited for the impending rush of friends and subjects, Valine started asking questions.

"What happened? Is everyone alright?"

I glanced at Dryden before looking back at her, and my chest tightened. "We lost quite a few men, including..."

Valine's fingers curled into fists, and she gritted her teeth as she said, "Tell me. Who didn't make it?"

I reached out a hand and wrapped it around her own. "I'm sorry, but Mordris didn't make it."

"No," she whispered, her eyes already reddening and filling with water once more.

I sniffled. "He was a good soldier and a great man."

Valine wiped her nose on her arm as Dryden rubbed his body against hers. "Yes. I will never forget him." She peered up, cheeks wet. "What about Zasper and Vashti? Citadel, Kasabian and Falchor? Please tell me they're all alright."

"They're alright," I replied.

Visible relief flooded through her as Valine's fingers swiped at her eyes, wiping away the tears. "Thank The Creator."

Yes. Indeed, despite all that had been lost, I was very thankful. My heart ached for Valine, knowing that she would be distraught over the loss of yet another comrade, but she was alive. Perhaps it was selfish of me, but I was so very grateful that she had survived. If she hadn't... Well,

I didn't have to imagine it now. My Little Bird was alive, and we could be there for each other through the mourning and grieving and whatever other trials laid ahead.

CHAPTER
NINETEEN
VALINE

I *woke up, my* mind groggy and my limbs heavy. I had
slept in, the most I had in a long time, but I still felt like
I could sleep for the whole day. What was wrong with me?
Why was I still feeling this way? I had thought it was the
after effects of the ice-induced long slumber, or perhaps
my body had been so worn down from everything the past
year that I had simply caught a seasonal illness. But it had
been three weeks, and I still felt the same. *Terrible.* Daily
headaches, muscle pain, and brain fog. I didn't even have
the energy to walk to the dining hall. I was so exhausted no
matter what I did, no matter how much I slept and rested.

A weight sunk into the bed next to me. Lux brushed the
hair from my face and stared down, worry lining his brow.
"How are you feeling today, Val?"

I tried to sit up, but quickly gave up, the movement
requiring too much energy that I didn't possess. I sighed,
collapsing back down into the mattress. "Still not well."

Lux's fingers absentmindedly rubbed my forearm. He
was always touching me—a finger wrapped around a curl

of hair, a hand holding mine, a knee leaning against my leg.

He sighed. "We should call for the court physician."

"No," I whined, "I don't want to bother him. I am sure I will feel better soon."

Lux frowned, his brows coming together. "You said that for weeks now. I am calling for him."

"Fine," I grumbled.

The physician came a few minutes later, since his quarters were in the same hall as my own; it was always useful for a monarch to have a healer nearby. He was tall and thin with a pointed nose and freckles dotting his skin. He pushed his glasses up as he set up his tools on the bed table.

Pregnancy, seasonal illness, and every known disease and disorder was ruled out via poking, prodding, and a plethora of questions about how I was feeling. Nothing was left out, even down to details of my bowel movements.

The physician rubbed his neck. "My apologies, Your Majesty. I cannot seem to identify what is ailing you."

Lux scolded, "How could you not know? Aren't you supposed to be the best healer in Racour?"

I reached out and squeezed his hand, knowing that his outburst was caused out of concern for me. "It's not his fault, Lux. Don't be hard on him." As the words left my mouth, my mind started to race, which did nothing to help my aching head, and my pulse quickened as I pondered what was the cause of my poor condition.

The physician spoke, "Perhaps... It has something to do with your slumber. I am not familiar with magic, but it may be that it has something to do with your ailments."

Lux's eyes widened, as we both recalled the battle in caverns, remembered the torture and torment that occurred. In fact, my headaches had started from my first meeting with Noctis and had only gotten progressively worse as time went on. Perhaps whatever perverse magic the Fallen had possessed and used on us was the reason for my poor health, but that didn't make any sense because the others who were there had reported no issues. It had to be something else then.

A sacrifice.

My mind drifted, hypothesizing what and why this was happening. Certainly this wasn't the sacrifice that the prophecy was referring to. That must have been fulfilled in my freezing of Noctis, and my coming back to life a gift, the pity of The Creator. There was no possible way that my health, that living a life of chronic pain, was what was being required of me.

I scribbled a letter to Zasper, the ink barely having time to dry before I folded it and sent it off with a servant. It would take the letter a few days to reach her, and the waiting was agonizing. I was so certain she could heal me, that if magic had caused the problem that magic could heal it too.

Only a day later my door opened to reveal my friend. I sat upright, in what felt like lightning speed to me but knowing how weakened I'd become likely was very slow. She gave me a smile that failed to reach her eyes.

Ignoring the pity in her gaze, I asked, "How did you arrive so fast?"

She strode towards the bed and sat, her hand wrapping around my own. "I was already on my way after hearing you had awakened and ran into the messenger on the road. I would have come sooner, but I had many things to attend to after being in Racour for so long."

I placed my other hand atop hers, sandwiching them between my palms. "Well, thank The Creator you are here. I can't lie, it's been a rough few weeks. I've been vomiting a lot and my legs feel like a newborn foal. No matter how much I sleep, I feel as if I haven't at all."

She nodded, her brows drawn down and her lips pursed. "I've never heard of something like this."

I forced out a hollow laugh. "Well, it's not everyday one has to fight a dark and magical entity and then spend months in an icy coma."

From his place on the opposite side of the bed, Lux nodded in greeting. "Thank you for coming. She is smiling now, but it's been hard for her."

Zasper's lips twitched up. "We should get to it then."

As I leaned back against the wall of my bed and exhaled, I closed my eyes. *Thank you that it is over, that I'll finally feel better.*

I felt her hands warm as they hovered and roamed over my body, but as soon as they moved the heat evaporated, replaced with an aching cold. Disappointment creeped around the corner, but I shoved it back. Everything was fine. It was just going to take some time.

Minutes passed, but still no change.

I opened my eyes to meet Zasper's own, and the sunlight pouring through the window reflected on a wet line that ran down her cheek.

"I-I'm sorry," she whispered, her tone weighed with defeat.

"What?" I asked, my heartbeat starting to pick up along with my pitch. "What do you mean? No. No. *No.*"

I lurched forward and grabbed her hands, yanking them over my legs. "Try again," I insisted.

Zasper gently tugged her hands free. "I don't think there is anything I can do."

The body aches and exhaustion still plagued me, and now I was devastated, my last hope ruined. I threw a glass at the wall, anger providing enough energy to do so, and the shattered remnants clinked to the ground. The maids winced and hastily moved to clean it up.

Zasper and Lux sat on my bed, sympathy mixed with an uncertainty of what to do in this moment.

"It's unfair! I have tried my best to live honorably, to obey the will of The Creator, and this is my reward? He ignores my pleas for healing. How is that *loving*?" I asked, venom and bitterness coating my voice.

I wanted to cry and shout to the heavens and demand answers. Why? Why was this happening to me? Wouldn't I be a better ruler, couldn't I be more valuable if I had my health back, if I could work hard developing my kingdom and helping the citizens instead of lying in bed all day? Tears fell down my face as a lump formed in my throat.

The lines of Lux's face turned hard, and he said nothing, his hand clasping my own in silence.

Zasper wrung her hands. "I'm sorry, *Chui*. But He is still good, still there, watching over you."

"That's easy for you to say. You have no idea what I am feeling, how bad everything hurts."

Zasper was about to speak again but thought better of it.

I whispered into the air, "I want to die. I don't want to live if this is how I will be for the rest of my life."

Lux sucked in a breath, his voice breaking. "Please don't say that, Val."

"Why?" I hissed. "How can I be a queen when I can't even focus during meetings? How can I rule from my bed?"

Zasper leaned forward, patting my leg. "It will get better."

I glared at her. "Don't say that. You don't know for certain."

She opened her mouth, but Lux interrupted, "Maybe you should leave us alone for now, Princess Zasper."

Zasper nodded and left without saying another word.

Good. I didn't want to hear it.

Lux laid down next to me, and I curled into his side. "It's not fair. It's not fair. *It's not fair*," I repeated through the sobs.

He kissed my forehead. "I know, Little Bird."

Zasper returned home, her magic offering no cure, and her words, no matter how well intentioned, were grating. And no matter how good their reputation, every healer we hired was unable to help.

"May I suggest that Your Majesty try exercising? It is good for both the mind and body," an expensive healer from Manchur offered.

"It's a little hard to exercise when everything hurts, and I don't even have the energy to walk down the hall," I grumbled, doing my best not to freeze his lips shut. Although my body was weak, my magic was still there, still eager to carry out my will.

"Well, it is possible that your symptoms are caused by your mind, and if you just press through for a while, things will improve," he replied in all seriousness.

How did this healer have such a good reputation? And how dare he assume it was all in my head? Of course, I was depressed since I was in pain, and many people didn't even believe me. Lux had overheard two servants whispering about how I was either lazy or crazy.

"I was walking down the corridor when I overheard two maids debating whether your ailments were real or if you were faking it," Lux explained. *"When I confronted them, they apologized, and of course, I accepted. Something strange happened though. Their garments caught fire all of a sudden, but don't worry, I put out the flames before any serious injury occurred."*

A mixture of gratitude and anger swirled inside me. They had no idea what it was like. I looked up at Lux from where he sat next to me on the sofa.

"Thank you," I whispered.

He smiled and leaned over to press his warm lips to my cold forehead. "Don't worry, they're no longer with us."

"You killed them?" I gasped.

Lux shook his head. "No, of course not. I just mean their jobs were terminated, and they were sent home."

I wrung my aching hands together. I was thankful that Lux not only defended me but also believed me, but there would be many who didn't. We couldn't just banish people from our presence all the time. Tears welled in my eyes. This was so unfair.

"Lux," I whispered with a burning cold, "escort this healer out of here before I send him back to Manchur as a frozen statue."

Lux mumbled something to the man as he rushed to get him out of the room, the renown healer having the audacity to look offended, his judgmental eyes looking back at me as he left. I looked down to my blanket, ice having crusted around my finger and intertwining with the threads of the fabric.

Lux and my attendants encouraged me not to give up, and we tried different diets—no meat this month, no grains the next—but no change ever helped. We tried different treatments such as pressure points, acupuncture, and disgusting daily tonics, but still my pain and exhaustion clung to me with a fierce reluctance to leave.

Eventually, I just grew tired of the suggestions, dreading the ultimate failure that would come of it. Nothing was working.

Having just finished a two week period in which I bathed every morning in freezing cold baths and drank a pitcher of reishi—some red tree fungus—and ginger tea, I was disheartened and refused to ever get near mushrooms again.

Steward Myra was nearby organizing some papers on my desk, suggesting a treatment that her mother-in-law had used back in the day for common colds.

"You sit outside in the sun for fifteen minutes right after after waking up, and then you eat 3 oranges a day," she finished explaining.

Sighing, I replied, "I think I need a break from trying new things."

She nodded, the smile she wore weighed down with pity. "I'm sure it will get better, Your Majesty."

I had come to loathe those words despite their good intentions as the sentiment did me no good, just as hope did me no good. It was far easier to accept that I would be like this until the day I was finally released from life, and my only practical anticipation was that I would get a new body in the afterlife.

Like tenderly nurturing and watering a precious plant, only for someone to come along and trample it, so was hope to me—a futile clinging to an uncertain promise that once collided with the harsh reality would only bring more despair than it having never existed in the first place. Acceptance was a far easier road to travel, and I wished people would allow me that without trying to force their own optimism that could only exist out of ignorance onto me.

I was already in so much pain and yet I did my best to be considerate, so I just replied, "Thank you."

It was easier to resign myself to my new reality rather than hold onto a false hope. This was my life now. Yet accepting that my new normal was one of aches and fatigue didn't take away the mental torment and despair.

Was this the sacrifice? Why couldn't I just have died? Giving up my health, living the rest of my life in pain, was too much for me to handle.

Later that night while Lux was absent, busy with a meeting in Aryll territory that was too far of a trip for me to handle, I prayed and prayed, got on my knees to beg as tears and snot poured down my face and my hand beat against my chest.

"Take me! Please take me! I can't live like this. What kind of life is this? Everything hurts, and I am tired of the pain. Do you despise me so much that you would rather see me suffer like this? Why won't you talk to me like you did with Egann? Where are the miracles that are written in the scrolls of old? I have done everything you asked. I may not be perfect, but I have never once not believed in you. Those who ignore you, who don't follow your ways, they are doing better than me. Why? What is the point of following you if you don't speak, don't answer me? What is the point of living if the rest of my days are tinged with sorrow and anguish?"

Dryden whimpered nearby, unsure of what to do as I beat my fists against the ground, my voice croaking as my throat clogged. "Why must I live? Why me? Just why?"

I leaned forward, pressing my forehead against the cool tile as my teardrops fell onto the floor. Dryden padded next to me and began rubbing his head against my back and side. I turned towards him, burying my face and hands into his fur.

I would take on your pain if I could, he muttered.

Could you please just kill me instead? I asked.

I don't understand your human humor, he growled.

I wasn't joking.

I was in a downward spiral. Down, down, down, into a dark pit of pain, suffering, and despair. That's all my world was anymore.

Lux burst into the room, rushing towards me. He yanked my sleeves up to reveal red lines that resembled cat scratches, intentionally too shallow to inflict life threatening damage.

"Val—" He choked back tears. "Oh my Little Bird," he rasped. Lux laid his head on my arm and cried.

With my other hand I reached over and ran my fingers through his hair. "I'm sorry," I whispered. "I just wanted to be in control for once, to be in charge of how I felt. I just... I just..."

"Where is Dryden? Why didn't he stop you?"

I couldn't meet his gaze as I replied, "I locked him outside."

Lux peered up at me, eyes red and watery. "Please, never again."

I nodded. "I promise."

But I broke my promise, unable to resist the urge to bring the blade to my wrists. Lux cried that time too. And the next.

I wasn't sure if he could understand why I did though.

I'd always prided myself on my strength and brain. I was stronger than most girls, and my mind was as sharp as a scholar's quill. But now I was a shell of my former self. I was tired no matter how much I slept, and my bones and muscles ached, as if someone had beaten me up. I wasn't strong or smart anymore. I had always been independent, but now... now I would need help. And I loathed myself for it.

"The physician said you could get better," Lux whispered in his attempt at encouraging me.

"He also said there was an equal chance that I wouldn't," I snapped.

I stared out the window longingly. I yearned to be outside, to be active, but my body had betrayed me, my youth stolen. No one knew for sure if I would get better, worse, or if this would simply be my new normal. The hope of a cure, of getting better, seemed to be too cruel, like a mirage of water in the desert. Would I ever get to drink from its refreshing spring? Or would I be cursed to crawl continually, just trying to survive. Lux gripped my hand and sat in silence as tears streamed down my cheeks.

I laid in bed, unable to sleep from the pain, from the pounding in my head and the sharp stabbing in my knees that were swollen and inflamed. I gazed at the ceiling as if it wasn't there, as if I could see past it all the way to the heavens. Forming was the familiar pressure in my chest and quivering of my chin as I whispered, water in my eyes and pleas on my lips, "I would do anything you asked of me. Am I doing something wrong? If there is something you want me to do, please just make it clear."

Then speaking out loud became too difficult, so I switched to praying in my mind. *Why do you ignore my prayers? Did I do something wrong? Egann said that you spoke to him, that he heard your voice, and others have said they've seen you in dreams and visions. But why not me? I have tried so very hard, worked so diligently, so why me? Why do I have to have this burden? Why won't you heal me? I know you can, which makes it hurt all the more that you refuse to. If you won't heal me, then please kill me. Make an end of my suffering. Will you allow me that at least?*

For weeks I imagined killing myself, a myriad of ways to cease my torment. Drown myself in the Xian River, jump from the palace roof, obtain a lethal amount of sleeping and pain tonics, or even wander into the mountains during a snowstorm and allow myself to be consumed by the elements. I never carried any of them out though. There were only two reasons that kept me from it: Lux and Dryden would be absolutely broken, and The Creator would be very sad to meet me in that way. It wasn't much, but it was enough to prevent me from doing it.

There was one small joy, one tiny thing to look forward to, an ember of light in my dark world.

I was expectantly waiting for the arrival of a gift from Princess Vashti, a rare and precious fruit—a Percian delicacy. She said that they were as sweet as honey when picked ripe and that the plants that grew them were so sensitive and temperamental that most of the buds died before fully forming. It may have seemed unimportant to most, but it was a raft to a shipwrecked man, a little spark of joy to hold onto amidst the turbulent waters of my life. It was the only thing I had to look forward to.

After weeks of waiting, a servant brought word that they had arrived, and I leapt to my feet, my knees protesting at the jarring movement. Ignoring my body aches, I rushed to the palace entrance and slipped through the main doors before the guards had a chance to fully open them. A wagon with a single crate surrounded by straw waited in the yard, and I dashed towards it, mouth already salivating at the thought of the sweet treat.

A servant that had accompanied the precious cargo bowed and pried open the box. I leaned over, fingers tapping together. Then they stilled, and my mouth turned down.

Maggots crawled around inside, white lines wriggling amongst the dark purple-red fruit.

I collapsed to the ground, shouts of dismay and concern emitting from servants and soldiers.

Myra, who happened to be near, rushed to my side. "Your Majesty, please don't cry. We can get more of the fruit."

My voice cracked as I spoke, "It's never about the fruit, Myra! It was one good thing, one thing that I was excited about, and even that was taken from me. One rock doesn't seem heavy, is bearable, but add twenty more and the weight becomes too much."

Perhaps there was something wrong with my expectations, that just because I suffered in one, or several ways, that that excluded me from any and all other problems. Yet that was not the way of things. Life was an ocean full of waves that crashed into you one after another, and they wouldn't cease just because one had slammed into you just moments before. Some days the water was calm while other times were filled with rough seas. I prayed I would get calm waters soon; I was tired of swimming.

That night, Lux was once again away handling state affairs in my stead, but this time Rosalva kept me company, Lux insisting that I not be allowed alone. At his behest, there was always someone present with me, a guard or servant, just to make sure I didn't do anything no matter how many times I insisted that I wouldn't do what they feared I would. A mixture of irritation and gratitude flowed inside me.

I curled into myself, wishing the soft pillows and blankets could seep into my body and soothe my aching muscles and joints, but soon the cushion beneath my head became wet, soaked with tears. My chest tightened and my fists clenched the pillow, indignation at the unfairness of it all, the hollowing feeling of abandonment by The Creator, and frustration that no matter what I did, nothing got better, all swirled together in my mind.

I choked out, "Is He punishing me? Did I do something wrong? I mean, I know I'm not perfect, but after all I've done, after how hard I have strived to help others, how can He do this to me? Am I not good enough? Why does He ignore me, shut out my cries?"

Rosalva stroked my hair and said, "Sometimes people don't get better and it's not a reflection of their faith or an indication of doubt, nor is it a punishment for some great wrongdoing. Sometimes, He withholds His hand, much to our chagrin. And He can make good come from it, from our pain and bad experiences."

"You know what's good? Not hurting, not losing your friends and family, not being sick," I grumbled.

How was this sickness good? How did such suffering do anyone any good? When I was on the run with my rebels, that trial was for something great, fighting evil, and when I was whipped by Hagan, at least that was inspiring—standing for what was right and saving another—but this... This helped no one.

Rosalva continued to run her fingers through my hair. "I know. It doesn't mean those things become any less hard, but they can make you kinder, more aware of the pain of those around you, and as a monarch, make you a better ruler."

I scoffed, asking, "Was I so bad before? Was I so despicable that I needed such severe chastisement?"

"It may not be about what you were but about who you would become. Perhaps He was helping prevent something, guiding you down a different path. Who knows, maybe somehow you would have become a tyrant, or at the very least arrogant and uncaring about your people. Sometimes the thing that feels like it will destroy us, is the very thing that will save us. The truth is, these are all just guesses, and we will never know why. Sometimes He leads us to still waters, other times to stormy seas, and both serve a purpose, even if we don't know it."

My body recoiled and stiffened at her words, indignance raging through me. But then I paused. Maybe she was right, and my pride was resisting her words.

Pondering what she said, I nestled my head in her lap as her wrinkled hands stroked my hair. I hated not knowing why. But would knowing the reasons change anything, cease the pain? No. Either way, it was hard to maintain faith, to hold onto hope, when one could not see the end, and I felt like I was blindly stumbling through a hallway with not the smallest speck of light.

CHAPTER TWENTY

VALINE

It had gotten back to the palace that some of the people of Racour were already whispering about their sovereign, condemning me as "Queen of Sleep" and "Ruler of Beds". Was this how my mother had felt? I wondered what was going on in her mind during her reign, if she had been aware of the people's opinion or willfully ignorant of it, or perhaps if her officials had purposefully kept her unaware. A knock on the door shook me from my thoughts as I let the reports I had been reading fall against the blankets.

"Enter," I called out, and a maid opened the door with a letter in hand.

She walked to the bed and handed the paper to me.

"Who is it from?" I asked.

The woman replied, "I am not sure, Your Majesty. It was left on the steps of the palace."

"Oh." I thanked and excused her, and as she left I inspected the mysterious letter. Turning the paper over, there were three words written: *For the Queen.*

I hadn't heard of anyone being assassinated via letter, although a topical poison applied to the paper would be a good way to go about it, but I wouldn't be so lucky as to die. I was certain I could be shot with an arrow through the heart and still somehow survive it—much to my chagrin.

I cracked the seal and unfurled it.

To Her Majesty, High Queen Valine,

Greetings, my sovereign. You do not know me, for I am but a simple woman in a small village. But I felt the need to write to you, to encourage you. Rumors reached even my humble community, and I heard you have been unwell for many months, that you are likely to continue to be in such a condition indefinitely.

How hard it must be, to be in such agony and yet no one can see it, no one can truly comprehend it.

I thought you might like to know that my chickens are molting. They do so every year for about two to three months, and their pretty feathers fall off, mostly just eating and sleeping without producing any eggs. But you see, I raised them from the moment they hatched, keeping them warm and safe, and I hand-fed them. I love them very much, even now, when they provide me with nothing in return. They offer no food nor very pretty to look at, yet they are just as lovely and special to me.

You probably think I am insane for using Your Grace's precious time to discuss chickens, but there is a reason for it.

You see, just as I love my chickens even when they can give nothing in return, so The Creator loves you. You may not feel that way right now, and I understand why.

However, I hope that you could be encouraged, find hope and comfort in this: your current sufferings are not the end, are nothing compared to the eternity of glory that awaits. Life can be cruel and unfair, and it can be hard to comprehend the ways of The Creator, but we aren't supposed to know everything, the why's and how's and when's. Although not the answer to your problems, there can be a comfort in letting go of control.

I am sorry that you are having to endure such hardship, as I am aware of how compassionate Your Majesty's heart is after all you've done to right the wrongs of both your mother and the previous king, but He can use your suffering too. It's not a punishment, although it is a great humbling—prevention of pride, as my father used to say—that can be used to help others. How exactly, I am not sure, but He knows. And it is said that suffering helps purify one, and if we allow it, can bring glory to The Creator which to those who have no faith, do not know His character, might find such methods selfish or unnecessary.

Even if Your Majesty must sign edicts in bed and delegate responsibilities to worthy advisors, it makes you no less a queen. Many a High Queen before have had trials, some emerging triumphant on the other side, others failing to stay true until the end. I pray daily that Your Grace would be the former.

It is normal to mourn, to grieve over lost dreams, lost relationships, lost health, but do not stay in such a state. Cry when you must, but do not forget to dry your tears and thank Him. From what I hear, your consort seems a doting and fine man. That in and of itself is a rarity. He gives and He takes away, but life is a lot better and filled with more joy if you choose to focus on what He has granted.

Don't be so hard on yourself if you can't lay eggs, Your Majesty. You're still loved.

That was it, no name, no indication of who the woman was. My cheeks were wet, and my chest was tight. I smiled with tears pouring out as I looked up to the ceiling, and for the first time in a long while, I thanked Him.

Even as I wept and mourned the loss of my health, my identity, and all the things I had dreamed of accomplishing but no longer could, I found myself able to also acknowledge the good, the blessings, and that internal shift felt like a door opening—an unexpected door that I never wanted—but it was a new chapter nonetheless. A new me.

Healing was a luxury that many did not have. It required time and money. Many people who suffered from some sort of disability or disease still had to work, couldn't afford a myriad of treatments from healers across Saego or have people to take care of them. I could lay in bed when needed, had servants to bring me things, had friends who were understanding and encouraging, and enough wealth to hire the best healers.

Thus, I did my best to be grateful, to thank The Creator for things big and small. Some days were easier and others harder, but there was always something to be grateful for, like Lux being willing to rub my aching knees or because there was a particularly delicious dish served that day.

I tried my best not to complain too much, anxious that my very real pain would be relegated to a pessimistic personality for those who couldn't see my daily struggles and the weeping as I lay in bed, my body feeling like it had been trampled by horses. I didn't want people to think of me as inept or lazy, but they could never comprehend how much effort it took to climb the stairs, my knees protesting with grinding pain, or trying to be decisive about an important proposed policy when my mind was fogged over.

Had I been missing a leg, no one would bat an eye, sympathy posed on the tip of their tongues, but my ailments were invisible, no proof to present to them of just how badly I suffered, and even if they never said it aloud, I could see the judgment in their faces, a roll of the eyes as I mentioned my aching muscles or a sigh as I joked that a storm was coming because my knees were as swollen as rain clouds. Many didn't take my illness seriously, including my officials.

My stewards, along with a few Pardus nobles, had gathered to petition, well more accurately insist, that Lux and I do a tour of the country showing our unity and strength to inspire our people.

Myra spoke, "It would encourage everyone that you are in good health, even if it is a façade, and that Racour is strong. In the south, some still fear retribution from Indo concerning the war. Even though peace has been declared, they still worry, but seeing their queen, with magic and dragons no less, would calm their nerves and solidify their trust in the crown."

Quilian Novarre, a noble who oversaw the trade in Pardus, stated, "I agree, Your Majesty. It will also assure everyone that the Queen and her consort are in love and that there is sure to be an heir in the near future."

I resisted the urge to roll my eyes and did my best to keep my voice calm. "I understand your reasoning, and I even agree to some extent. However, at this time, I will not be conducting a tour." Maintaining the façade of normality during these few meetings was draining enough as it was.

Quilian argued, "But, Your Majesty, it is essential to instill trust into the people. I am sure there are still many who are worried that you will be like your mother. Even more rumors have spread that you are spending a significant amount of time in bed, and an increasing number of people are becoming concerned that you are indifferent to ruling. It is, after all, impossible to keep every servant and soldier from talking about such things. Gossip spreads like wildfire, and it may just consume your reign if you don't put it out."

I scoffed, leaning back against my throne. "After all I have done to rid this kingdom of Vukan? Have I not proven myself already? I've lowered taxes, encouraged the employment of more women, spent resources investigating the women he kidnapped, and have strengthened international ties." I had read the reports, but back then it was a minute amount of Racourians. Now it seemed to slowly be shifting to the majority.

He shifted, eyes darting to the others in the room. "People are quick to forget the good things and even quicker to think poorly of others. If you wish to put an end to these whispers, then I suggest you reconsider our proposition."

My hands gripped the arms of my throne, my fingernails digging into the carved wood. "Do you know what it's like," I asked, my voice a hard whisper, "for your body to feel like it has been crushed by a boulder, for your head to feel the throbbing pressure of a thousand stones, and for your mind to become thick and sticky like mud? Do you know the feeling of being betrayed by your own body, weak in the era of youth when one is supposed to be at their peak? Do you see the judgmental looks and hear the comments made by those older in the court, that I can't be tired and my joint's can't possibly be hurting because I am young? Do you know what it is like to be a prisoner in your own body?"

Silence. Because of course they didn't.

Only those who had chronic ailments, and sometimes those who lived with them and had to take care of them, could possibly know. At our very beings, humans were unable to comprehend most things unless they directly affected their lives. I was guilty of such prejudice myself, having often thought of others as weak or lazy when they had battles raging under the surface. I had ignored people who were drowning, and instead of helping them out of the water, I had told them to learn to swim. How foolish and arrogant I had been. I had much growing to do, and just like a tree, the pruning process was painful.

Lux could understand though, and on one brisk spring morning, he'd revealed more of his past to me.

Frost had tinted the glass, blurring the budding cherry blossoms outside. We had been laying next to each other in bed, soaking in each other's presence.

"Did you know I have headaches too?" Lux had asked with a soft voice as his finger drew lines on my shoulder.

I had snuggled tighter into the crook of his arm, guilt gripping my insides. I scolded myself for never asking how he was. He had suffered in that cave too, had been suffering at the hand of his father long before that, yet I never asked about his pain.

"I'm sorry," I whispered, squeezing him tight. "Would you tell me about it?"

"Despite him beating me as a child, I always chased his approval, sought his love. It was as pointless as trying to capture the wind. I could never be as cruel as he desired, and I think he saw too much of my mother in me, who had escaped from him. Since he could no longer torment her, could not take out the rage at her audacity for leaving him, he turned it to me. Once when I was about seven, he beat me in my head, and ever since, I've always had aching in my skull."

His shirt beneath my cheek had grown wet, salt kissing my lips. "Oh, Lux..." I rasped. "I don't know what to say, but I love you. I'm here for you, too. I want to take care of you just as you do me."

From above my head, he sniffled. "I love you, Little Bird. I'm just grateful that you came to end my nightmare."

"We can be each other's dream," I said, tilting my head up to kiss his cheek.

Warmth had bloomed in my chest as my hand rested against his. The Creator had blessed me with such a kind and patient man. Perhaps that was his mercy, that if I had to suffer, I wouldn't be alone, would have a safe person who would hold me when I cried and complained without a hint of judgment.

As for the rest, I could get a week, a month, maybe even a year of sympathy before they grew tired of dealing with my illness, tired of hearing how my legs hurt, tired of me canceling a meeting because everyday was uncertain in the severity of my pain and sometimes I had to rest instead of fulfilling previous appointments.

On top of that, although my mental state had improved, I struggled with feelings of being a burden, both physically and financially. Lux and the stewards would have to work extra hard as I was unable to meet every demand and responsibility of being ruler, and the people, it felt unfair of me to spend so much money on hiring more staff and inviting expensive healers from around the continent to attempt to cure me—not even a guarantee that I would get better.

I exhaled, my grip on the throne relaxing. "I will not be going on tour at this time. Creator willing, I will be feeling better in the summer. Until then, I do not want to hear another word concerning this topic."

They all bowed and replied in unison, "Yes, Your Majesty."

A country-wide trip would take too much of my precious health, and if all that I had done, and planned to do from my throne, were not enough to win the favor and faith of Racourians, then a tour wouldn't either. There was a smaller trip I wanted to make though.

CHAPTER TWENTY-ONE

LUX

I *woke up with* the taste of salt in my mouth and wetness in my ears. The remnants of my nightmare were fading, but I could still picture the obsidian fangs and blue veins, feel the cold and rough blade slice my arm, could hear the piercing screams of my wife as she writhed on the stone floor of the cavern. I felt a hand slide over my chest.

"Another bad dream?" Valine asked, her voice husky and her eyes slowly blinking open.

I nodded, pulling her closer.

"Vukan?"

"Noctis," I muttered, chills still crawling through me at the thought of him.

She pressed her lips to my cheek. "Don't worry. This is real. We are here—together."

Turning my head, I inhaled, the scent of roses and persimmon filling my nose. Valine was here. We were safe.

"You should probably get ready for court," I said, untangling myself from her. I stared at her, my hand moving to her face without a thought, my fingers caressing her cheek. "I'll meet you afterwards for lunch."

I slipped my arms through the wide sleeves of my robes, tying a sash around my waist. Glancing back at her one last time before leaving, I shouted, "I love you."

Her nose scrunched together as she smiled and replied, "Love you too. See you later."

As I closed the door behind me, I nodded to the guards stationed in the hall and gave Dryden—who had started sleeping out in the hall in order to give us privacy—a quick scratch on the snout before walking down the hallway.

I headed out towards the coves of trees on the mountain side of the palace. The smell of evergreens and chirping of birds filled the air. I let out a low and long whistle.

Rustling above me and flashes of emerald and cobalt scales gave away the location of the dragons. I heard a snap and had just enough time to catch the blue bundle as Bahm crashed towards the earth. He landed in my arms with a smack, and my knees shook from the impact.

Looking down at him, I scolded, "I told you not to try climbing trees yet. You still aren't used to gliding with three legs."

Sol landed with a soft thump on the grass, her violet eyes iridescent in the sunlight that peaked through the small cove.

"And you were supposed to make sure he listened," I chided.

Her only reply was a cock of her head.

Chuckling, I crouched down until I felt the ground beneath me, Bahm settling into my lap as his sister curled beside my thigh.

Exhaling, I leaned back against the tree, the bark rough against my back. Every time I came here, I was reminded of her song, of the afternoon in which she had been betrayed and abandoned by Sebastien. Although I was glad I was with Valine, I wished it wasn't due to his skewed philosophies. At first, I had thought it was my fault, that not letting him see my father's wrath when we were children had made him ignorant to his cruelty, but even as an adult, even after seeing the vile things he ordered, my cousin had refused to be anything but filial to his family and king.

Gazing towards the mountains, I wondered where he was, how he was doing. I lifted a prayer to the skies, hoping he was well, that he would live the best he could with what he was given.

Bringing my eyes back down, each hand stroking the scales of my dragons, I dared to imagine what the future would be like. Now that I was no longer just surviving, I could dream about how to live.

I didn't know what I could do to help her. My love alone was not enough to heal her, to save her from her pain. I wanted to cry, to punch a wall, to scream, and ultimately none of it mattered in the sense that I couldn't take her pain away, to restore her body to what it was before. I did the best I could though, to handle the matters that were of less importance, to rub her head, shoulders, knees, or whatever else was particularly painful that day. It felt like holding a cloth to a gaping wound, slowing the bleeding but not fixing the problem.

She had been through so much already, and even more so now, and I was amazed at her strength and spirit.

There were moments where I, too, got tired and weary of the daily things required of me both from the nation and my wife, but I could never voice it. I knew that if I complained, it would be as good as stabbing her in the heart with a poison tipped dagger. She struggled with thoughts of being a burden, of being loathed for her illness. For the most part, I handled it well, but some days I wanted to rest, even daring to wish this wasn't the reality.

Even with a palace of servants, it was draining, but I didn't think anyone could understand the strange state I was in. They would probably call me selfish, cold-hearted, and ungrateful, seeing as I was her enemy's son—no one would have questioned her or batted an eye if I had joined my father in his execution—so I never spoke aloud my own grievances and fatigue.

My sweet wife had encouraged everyone in the palace to treat me with respect as her consort, threatening those who needed a little extra convincing. She would not allow for an unkind word towards me.

Of course I didn't regret it, being with her, but when she was in severe pain, sometimes her tone and words were harsh, and no matter how many times I told myself not to take it personally, I couldn't help but feel sad—hurt—by it. I never held it against her, and I loved her, chose her, because love was a choice.

It wasn't your stomach fluttering in excitement from quick glances, or the sparks of a kiss, or even the roaring blaze of pleasure from sleeping together. Those were affection, passion—emotions that came and went—but love, love was growing old together, wiping the vomit from the other's mouth, choosing to apologize no matter how strong the internal sense of righteousness was, a devotion completely separate from one's feelings. Everyday I chose her and she me. We would choose each other until we grew gray and old, and even then, with wrinkled faces, hunched backs, and poor vision, she would still be the most breathtaking woman to ever grace the world.

Just as she was now, magnificent as she sat upon her throne, lavender robes spilling around her and gold crown nestled upon her head.

I watched her, her mouth turned up in a grin and eyes squished together. If one who was unaware of her condition were to see her now, they would be fooled by her façade, fooled into thinking she was fine, but I knew she wasn't, that behind that smile held a bottomless pit of pain—both physical and mental—and that she likely was longing to return to her quarters to rest. She never let them see her falter, let the anguish be perceived unless you were close to her. At least once a week she would cry, the crushing pain in her body and the fatigue that dragged her down unbearable, and yet bear it she did. She would sob into my arms, and I would hold her and just listen.

Just yesterday, upon entering the room and seeing the pink nose and red, puffy eyes, I knew it was one of those nights. Without saying a word, I padded over to the bed and climbed in, holding my arms open. She scooted across and snuggled into my chest, and I wrapped myself around her as my clothes gradually grew wet.

I knew there were no words to say, nothing that she wanted to hear—nothing that could change the way things were, so I just lay there as she cried out the frustration, pain, and exhaustion. No platitude could possibly bring an end to it; it simply sucked. My hand stroked her hair, and I nestled my cheek to the crown of her head, whispering prayers as I held her. What a sorrowful life she had been tasked with, but the bravery in which she faced it was beautiful. My Little Bird, even with injured wings she managed to sing.

Once she was done, she would wipe her tears, pray, and move on. Sometimes she would ask me to rub her head in order to ease the throbbing or massage her knees that ached. But I never saw those red lines on her arms again, and I would do anything to make sure they never returned.

She rarely complained despite the inner turmoil—never gave up. I stared at my Little Bird on her throne with complete adoration, my chest swelling with pride and gratitude. She caught me staring, and her smile widened even more, eyes sparkling.

The people could write her off as another entitled and lazy queen who couldn't bother to get out of bed many days, and the thought of that caused my flames to roar to life. But I knew. Anyone who saw her on a daily basis, who knew the terrible pain she was hiding behind her kind smile and warm eyes, who saw her collapse from exhaustion and cry from the agony, we knew who she was. So even if the people didn't—couldn't—recognize the victory it was for her to get up each morning, to fight a lifetime of internal battles, I would, and I'd tell her every single day how proud I was of her, how radiant and courageous she was.

Finally, she finished her business and excused the court. She gripped her purple layered skirts in her hand as she scurried over to me, eyes twinkling.

"Ready for lunch?" She asked, hand outstretched.

I took it on my own and leaned down to press my lips to her knuckles. "I'd prefer to skip to dessert," I replied, eyes dancing with a mischievous fire and a corner of my mouth curled to one side.

Valine rolled her eyes, but her smile remained as she linked her arm around mine. "You remind me of a certain Crown Prince."

"Oh, was he dashing and handsome?" I asked, watching her from the corner of my eyes.

"Deliciously," she said with a wink. "But not as delicious as the food I am going to make for us," she added, her speed picking up as we headed towards the kitchens.

I sat across from her, my eyes frozen to her beautiful figure. I loved everything about her, her eyes, her laugh, her tenacity, even her stubbornness. She'd insisted on cooking lunch for us, no servants, no help, just her. I sat in the kitchen with her, watching her attempt to cook with ingredients she had never seen in their raw form as most of her adult life spent eating wild game and boiled plants. Even after she was captured and brought to the castle almost two years ago, every meal was prepared by the servants. The bacon that she was attempting to fry was beginning to darken at the ends.

"Don't you think you should turn them over?" I asked, amusedly watching her scramble to cook multiple things at once.

She shook her head, a droplet of sweat sent flying as she replied, "I think it's fine."

A few moments later when she finished plating everything, I did my best to suppress a laugh at the sight of the near black pork.

Her hand jutted out, and she shoved a piece into her mouth, the crunching loud enough for the whole palace to hear.

"I-I like it this way," she said in between chomps.

I couldn't hold back the laugh anymore. "I'll make sure to remember how you like your bacon and make it that way for you in the future," I said with a wink.

I could see her mind working, the battle between her pride and the desire for actual, well-prepared bacon wrestling. Gosh, I loved her. We may irritate each other at times, but I would never trade her for the world. No matter what lay ahead, I was thankful for the loyal and brave woman before me, even if that loyalty was what would cause her to eat burnt bacon the rest of her life. Her commitment almost admirable.

My mother would have loved her.

CHAPTERTWENTY-TWO

VALINE

As *we exited through* the main palace doors, I looked up. A carved silver obelisk was set up at the main entrance to the palace with names engraved from top to bottom: *Ariella Polaris, Yanish & Fron Kobev, Callar Havis, Sokah Jang, Egann, Mordris Palvor*, and on and on the list went, a reminder to all who came and went, of what it took to gain peace and the sacrifices to maintain it. Even if they didn't know how they perished, at least their names would not be lost.

As we rode on our horses into town, Tempest relishing being outside the stables, we passed by the women's shelter. It was a new building with royal soldier's on duty at all times—an all female unit. The shelter was for all the women who were found during the investigations into Vukan's kidnappings. There, they would be allowed to receive protection, a place to live in the event that they didn't desire to, or couldn't, go home. They would have access to the best physicians as well as occupational training in a multitude of fields. The search had proved less fruitful than I had initially hoped, but I was still happy that a few had been located and rescued from their brothels. Soon it would be expanded and opened to any woman who was leaving an abusive situation.

I nodded to the female guards standing outside as we continued on our way.

My shoulders dragged low, and my chest was tight on top of the normal pain, dread filling me at the responsibility lying before me. Some of the larger house estates had accommodations for their servants on their land, but since she worked for a lower noble's house, her own quarters were in a different area of Pardus.

The building had three levels to it, with stairs climbing the side of the building leading to two doors. According to the information the stewards had provided, she would be on the third floor. I walked up the stairs, my feet feeling heavier with each step. I stopped in front of a wooden door with peeling red paint, a small window next to it, ivory orchids nestled on the sill.

Inhaling, I steeled myself for what had to be done—what was long overdue, and I doubted Vukan had even bothered to inform Zenith's mother of her death. Even if she had already come to the conclusion, it was only right to confirm it, to provide closure. I curled my fingers into a sweaty fist and knocked softly on the door. As my hand made contact with the wood, a wave of nausea washed over me, but I urged everything to stay put.

Muffled shuffling emitted from the home, and the door opened with a groan, a short woman with reddish brown hair and freckles, wrinkles lining her mouth and eyes, peered at me.

She had an apron over her dress, and flour dust floated to the ground as the women wiped her dough covered hands on the cloth. "How can I help you?" she asked, voice soft, much like her daughters had been.

I stuttered, a lump having formed in my throat, "M-ma'am. I am Queen Valine Polaris—"

Her eyes widened as she blurted, "Oh! Your Majesty." Her knees bent to bow, but I caught her elbow.

"No need," I said with a half smile. "May we come in?"

The woman nodded and mumbled, her voice shaking, "Of course. Please, Your Grace." She stepped back and gestured inside.

I nodded as I entered, Falchor and Lux trailing behind me. I hadn't wanted to draw attention with a large retinue, and I had ordered Citadel to wait downstairs, not wanting to overwhelm the woman.

She directed us towards the table and chairs, and the only other furniture was a stove, wash bin, and bed tucked in the corner behind a curtain. We sat at the table, careful to avoid the dolled out dough. The woman's face reddened, and she tucked some stray hair behind her ear. "What brings Your Majesty here?" she asked, picking at the dough pasted on her fingers.

I wanted to look away, but I refused to avoid her gaze, determined to give her the honor of at least that. It would be best to just get to the point, no need to draw it out. "I'm so sorry. I should have done this much sooner. Zenith is gone."

The woman crumpled to the floor, chair tipping over and tears streaming. "No!" she wailed.

I stood from my seat and bent beside her, unsure how to comfort her. "She was killed last fall by Vukan. I-I am sorry for your loss."

Weeping racked her body as cries of deep grief emitted from her throat. Her fists pounded against me, and I gritted my teeth. Falchor stood abruptly, but a shake of my head kept him away.

Once the sobs had turned to soft sniffles, I guided Zenith's mother up and helped her sit. Her face was puffed as a fresh pastry, and a dull glaze had settled over her eyes, one that I recognized all too well. I glanced at Lux and waved him forward. He leaned over the table towards us, a pouch in one hand. His eyes darkened, and I knew he was feeling guilty, as we both recalled that terrible day.

His voice was soft as he spoke, "I am forever sorry for your daughter's passing. And I know it can never replace her, but it's all I can do." He set the coin filled bag in front of her, and she finally looked up at him.

Her gaze hardened and her lips curled in disgust. "You're his son, aren't you? The Crown Prince Wulfric." Her hand grabbed the coins, anger blazing in her eyes. She launched the pouch at him, and he narrowly avoided being hit, coins scattering and clinking to the ground. "You can help by killing yourself and ending that cursed line!" she screamed.

Lux winced but said nothing. My blood heated, as I was torn between trying to respect the mourning mother's sorrow and protecting my husband from undeserved hatred.

I laid my hand gently atop of hers. "We are both sorry for your loss, and trust me, I know what it is like to lose loved ones, but I do ask that you respect the Prince Consort. He is innocent in this matter." A pang of pity rang in my heart, as I felt bad for both of them. I stood and moved next to Lux. "If the crown can do anything for you, please come to the palace and ask for Steward Myra. She will relay your needs to me."

Zenith's mother was silent, red eyes glued to the window sill that held the flowers. I took it as our cue to leave, and we walked towards the door.

Before I exited I heard Zenith's mother whisper, "She was supposed to come see the orchids. She is always too busy to visit me."

I closed the door behind us, leaving her to grieve her daughter, praying peace would come to her after her period of mourning. I held Lux's hand as we descended the creaking stairs to where Citadel was waiting with our horses, Tempest snorting as the Legate gripped the leather reins.

Before mounting, I paused, my hand going to my stomach. Lux appeared next to me, a soft hand clutching my elbow.

"Val, are you alright?"

My cheeks bubbled, and I shoved him away as I bent over, expelling the contents of my stomach. I coughed, the sour taste burning in my throat and mouth.

I wiped my lips. "I will be fine. I just need to get through today," I mumbled as I hooked my foot into the stirrup and swung myself into the saddle.

Next was the Jang residence. As difficult as informing Zenith's mother was, this would be a thousand times harder.

My hand hovered just above the wooden door, guilt gnawing at my insides. If only I had disregarded Zasper's words all that time ago, if only I had frozen Vukan's body as I had Noctis, even if I had ended up being killed... But there was no going back. What was done was done.

I knocked on the door to the quaint farmhouse, sweat pooling in my palm. A young girl opened the door, and tears blurred my vision.

The girl cocked her head and asked, "Are you okay?"

I sniffled, wiping my nose on my sleeve. "Are you parents here?"

The girl smiled, her lips favoring her right side with a small dimple in her cheek. "They are in the dining room. Come on in."

This time Citadel joined us too, the horses tied to a post outside. We entered the home and followed the girl into the dining area. It was more glamorous than Zenith's mother's house had been, but nothing compared to the luxurious palace. Forest green curtains hung in the windows, perhaps an ode to their family's origin being Roh territory, and an intricately woven rug lay beneath the maple table.

An old man with wispy facial hair and a woman with long dark tresses sat at the table laughing. The girl bounced to her parents and pointed at us with excitement. "Mama, Baba, we have visitors!"

Her parents looked at us, taking note of the ice leopard insignia of the soldiers' armor, and gasped, both immediately standing and stooping into a deep bow. "Your Majesty, to what do we owe this honor?" Sokah's father asked.

His mother yanked on her daughter's elbow as she scolded, "Minyoung, show respect to the queen."

Minyoung's eyes widened and her mouth formed an 'o' shape before she scrambled into a clumsy bow.

I waved my hands in the air. "Please, rise."

Sokah's father whispered to his wife, "Hyesun, go get some of the honey and ginseng tea we have been saving."

Hyesun nodded enthusiastically. "Yes, yes! Good idea, Jun."

I reached an arm out, as if I could block her path from so far. "No need for that." I lowered my hand, fingers rubbing my silk skirt together. "I, um, have come to deliver some news. You should sit."

The family scurried to sit, Hyesun pulling her daughter's sleeve until she situated herself next to her mother. Jun wrapped his arm around his wife, and my heart ached as I wiped my sweaty palms on my garments.

I gestured to the empty chairs. "May we sit?"

They both exclaimed in unison, "Oh yes! Of course. Please, Your Grace."

I smiled weakly. "Thank you."

Tucking my skirts beneath me, I sat, Lux taking the seat next to me while Citadel and Falchor took up positions behind us, a heavy purse in each hand. It was nothing compared to the life of their son, of my friend, but it was all I could offer as compensation.

Folding my hands, fingers clenched together until my knuckles changed color, I took a deep breath and delivered the news that would break the serene family in front of me. "I am sorry to inform you that your son has died."

Jun's hands gripped the table with the fury of all the stars, and Hyesun's cries cracked the air, but Minyoung, she just sat there, staring blankly into nothingness. Jun's anger turned into grief as he clung to his wailing wife, and still Minyoung just sat there frozen.

Obscured by the table, Lux's hand rested on my leg like an anchor to keep me steady. My eyes and nose stung, and my chin quivered, my voice cracking. "I am so sorry. I failed to protect him."

Because of me—because their son was a good man who intervened to save me—they had one less child. They would never see him get married or have kids. I readied myself for the barrage of hatred and sorrow to be thrown at me, but it never came.

Jun mumbled, tears streaking his cheeks, "I'm sure it's not Your Majesty's fault. We urged him not to sign up for the army, but that blasted boy didn't listen, enticed by the coin that we needed to pay off our debts. I should've forbade him from joining."

Hyesun paused her sobs to look up at her husband, hiccupping between each word. "No dear, it isn't your fault either."

He stroked his wife's head as he spoke, "We thought he had been sent on a mission, but this whole time he really…" Jun buried his face into Hyesun's hair.

Minyoung finally spoke, her words soft, "Sokah isn't coming back?"

My heart felt like it would implode, as if a hand had reached into my chest, squeezing until it would burst. I dug my fingers into my thigh, as if I could dispel the pressure into it.

Hyesun pulled her daughter into her embrace. "No sweetie, he isn't coming home."

Minyoung sniffled, and the tears broke through, pouring down her face. "I want my brother," she mumbled through quivering lips.

Hyesun patted her lap, and Minyoung crawled on her legs, her parents holding her tightly.

I moved my hand to Lux's, squeezing it, while beckoning Falchor and Citadel with the other. They approached, setting the coin bags on the table.

"It is nothing in repayment for his loyalty, for his life, especially when he saved mine, but he asked me to take care of you. I intend to honor that request, and anything that you could possibly need, do not hesitate to inform me. I know... I know it doesn't heal the pain, but—"

Jun, still embracing his wife and daughter, insisted, "You have nothing to repay or to make up for."

I glanced towards Lux, the couple's eyes following suit.

Hyesun was the one to speak first, "We do not blame His Highness either. If you have him by your side, then that speaks to his character. When we go into town, we often pass by that new women's shelter. And you even came personally to inform us about... about Sokah. I trust that Your Majesty is a good person."

The words elicited an unexpected response, and Lux broke into sobs, leaning into me. "Thank you. Thank you for saying that," he managed to say through the weeping.

I wrapped one arm around him, throwing off decorum. My other hand pressed against my chest, as if I could knead out the tightness. Seeing my husband weep brought out my own sobs that I'd been trying to hold in.

We all cried, mourned, and found some comfort in each other, and even Falchor had tears and snot streaming down his face.

"He was a good soldier and a great friend," he cried out.

Jun looked at me. "You said he saved you. Would you tell us about that?"

I coughed, dislodging the lump in my throat before replying, "It would be my honor." I paused, my head turned towards Sokah's sister, "I'm not sure if you'd like Minyoung to—"

She interrupted, her chin tilted up and lips stiffening, "I want to hear it."

Hyesun glanced at her husband, and after he nodded she whispered into her daughter's ear, "If it is too much, you can go to your room."

Minyoung nodded, her posture straightening in her mother's lap.

My hand found Lux's under the table as I regaled what happened over a year ago, "Back when I was a prisoner in the palace, Vukan had arranged for a sick game, a tournament in which the palace guards fought each other. Eventually he grew bored of even that twisted entertainment and demanded that these two young men fight until the death. I–I couldn't allow that to happen, refused to watch idly, so I spoke up. In retaliation, Vukan had me whipped. I probably would have died from it too, except that a brave, shining hero came to save me."

I had to pause to gather myself, my words catching as I knew what happened next, my head downcast. Jun and Hyesun scooted closer, arms wrapping even tighter around their daughter.

"Vukan was enraged, and in order to punish us both for insolence, he had Sokah hanged in front of me."

A small voice squeaked, "What were his last words?"

I jerked my head up and muttered, "Long live the queen."

A cacophony of cries burst forth once more, and we spent the next few hours talking about Sokah, of the lives he had touched, from helping an elderly neighbor milk her cow to teaching some young boys how to use a hammer and nails. Falchor and Citadel retold stories of nights out at the local tavern and Sokah's pranks on some of his fellow soldiers.

As I listened to the tales of the goofy guard, I smiled. I had not known him long, but he had left a mark in my life, in so many others, that would not be forgotten.

We laughed and cried and laughed again until the sun began to set.

When we left, the gushing flow of tears had slowed to a trickle, and I felt... better. I still missed him, still could envision his hanging body, but there was some sort of healing, a feeling of just being a bit lighter, the ache a bit duller.

As we once more mounted our horses, I asked, "What did Ferrum and Talom say, Falchor?"

Eyes averting my gaze, he replied, "They said their mother didn't wish to see you yet. They wish to mourn alone."

I nodded, unable to keep the hurt from my voice. "I see."

Falchor added quickly, "But they said their mother doesn't hold anything against you, just that she isn't ready to meet Your Grace, but later, she would be honored to speak with you."

I exhaled, hands curling around the reins. "Understood. Make sure to pass on that they are welcome anytime to the palace, and if there's anything they need that they can ask."

Falchor saluted. "Yes, Your Majesty."

CHAPTER TWENTY-THREE

VALINE

Lux and I sat on the sofa in our quarters without saying a word, Dryden purring as I ran my fingers through his fur while Lux had Sol and Bahm, with a healed stump where his leg had been torn off, snuggled around him. I was feeling better these days, well not physically, but mentally I was in a much better state. I knew there would be hard days ahead, but as I stared at Lux, I wasn't so worried or overwhelmed.

"What's going on in that head of yours? Scheming up some great plan?" he asked with a grin.

"I know everyone thinks I am a genius," I said as I flipped my hair over my shoulder, "and they're not wrong." I winked at him, and his lips curled up in response, amusement glittering in his eyes. I turned away as I spoke the next words, my voice heavy, "But I didn't know what to do after my comrades—my friends—were killed. I felt so lost, unsure what to do or where to go. Of course it all worked out, but that time was so hard, so confusing, like I was in a boat without an oar trying to go upstream."

A hand enveloped mine, and I looked up to see Lux intently studying me, his eyes that had been so bright a moment ago now a soft ember, barely glowing. I reached up with my other hand and touched his cheek. He placed his palm over mine, his thumb stroking my knuckles.

"I don't know why things happened the way they did, don't understand why so many good people died, but one good thing that came out of that darkness was you."

I leaned forward and closed my eyes, my lips brushing his.

It was a brief encounter, and as I pulled away I could see the fire light back in his eyes.

He grinned, his hand that had been holding mine now shifting to my mouth, his thumb whispering against my bottom lip, his gaze slowly crawling up to my eyes.

"I know that you have been surrounded by great darkness, but you have always shone with a brilliant light within it. You never cease to amaze me."

My heart danced inside my chest, and I felt my face warm as it was certainly turning red because even after all this time, he still made my heart flutter.

He cocked his head and lifted a brow as he said, "I hope you're not wishing you were with someone else."

My heart dropped a bit. Did he believe that I still was in love with Sebastien, or that I desired to be with someone else? Certainly he wasn't jealous of Kas? My hand drifted towards his, my fingers curling around his. "I love *you*. I chose *you*."

The corners of his mouth tipped up, and his words were coated with mischief. "You know why you and Sebastien could never work out?"

"Why?" I asked with a smile, prepared for some humorous quip, but I was shocked by the serious look in his eyes.

"Because he wanted a house-cat when you were born to be a leopard, and he would never have been able to handle you in all your magnificence. He had a preference for you when you were confined to your cage, but I prefer to see the leopardess in all her might." He leaned over, his hand slipping out from under mine and wrapping around the back of my neck as he pulled me forward and kissed my forehead. "I don't want you behind or beneath me, I want to be by your side, discuss things—make decisions together. I don't need glory nor power, just you."

I stared at his eyes, those delicious chocolate pools. "You know, the husband of the High Queen has only had the title of Prince Consort, but I wouldn't mind shirking tradition and changing that to King Consort."

Lux shook his head. "I'm not talking about that. I mean concerning the things of us—our relationship. I want us to be able to work together, choose together, like children, pets, where we go on vacation, things like that."

I smiled. "Well that is certainly less paperwork."

While gazing at him, I also couldn't help but notice how handsome he was. The shape of his jaw and the point of his eyes, and the way his nose rounded and the way his long hair fell down his back. My mind wandered, beginning to imagine him that night Zasper and I found him in an altercation with Sebastien.

I'd seen that back multiple times and this point, but no matter how often I saw it, it always had the same effect on me. My cheeks turned red, and my heart was pounding as loud as a gong and I wouldn't have been surprised if Lux could hear it. Heat crawled up my neck, and my limbs tingled. I bit my lip, and his hand fell and crept slowly down until it grazed my leg. I sucked in a breath and looked up to see Lux's eyes ablaze as he peered at me. His gaze dropped to my lips, and he leaned ever so slightly in my direction. I took it as an invitation, and closed the distance between us, our lips colliding. I loved kissing him, and I looked forward to a lifetime full of them.

The past many months had been filled with turmoil and struggle, but now that things had settled down and my mental state had improved, although the fatigue and aches persisted, I was excited for the future—*our* future.

His lips were warm and his hands soft as they crawled up my back and entangled into my hair. My own hands, as if they had a mind of their own, leapt to his torso and wrapped around it as they had so many times before the past few months. What felt like no time at all, we pulled apart panting, our lips upturned and eyes dancing.

I glanced at Dryden and ordered, *Take the dragons outside, please.*

I couldn't be certain, but I swore Dryden rolled his eyes—or an ice leopard's version of one—as he got up and corralled the dragons towards the door. He had gotten used to this, but he still complained about dragon sitting. I sent a whirlwind of ice to close the door, and it slammed shut. Just for good measure I froze over the handle.

Lux was staring at me perplexed, head tilted and brow cocked.

"Perhaps," I suggested coyly, "we should move to the bed."

Lux moved swifter than a deer, one arm bracing behind my back and the other tucking under my knees as he swept me into his arms and laid me gently on the bed. "I love you, Little Bird."

I craned my neck to kiss his lips and pulled back to whisper, "I love you, Lux."

The next morning, the sun was shimmering through the window, and I shifted towards Lux. His back was still bare, and with a finger, I traced the tattoo on his back. The two dragons were what I concluded were Sol and Bahm with a name in the center that I could only assume belonged to his mother.

He turned over, blinking the sleep away and speaking, voice groggy, "Good morning."

I chuckled and gave a soft kiss to his cheek. "You're adorable in the morning."

He yawned. "You've woken up beside me many times."

I smiled. "But you look so handsome everyday I don't think I'll ever get used to it."

A smile tugged at his lips, but was unable to fully form as if his face was still half-asleep. "Shall we repeat what happened last night?" he asked.

"Unfortunately, duty calls," I said as I threw the blankets off. I turned to look at him, winking as I promised, "But I'll take you up on that offer tonight."

Lux stretched, accentuating the lines of his forearms that I found particularly exciting to look at. "I look forward to it."

It had been a few weeks since visiting the families of my deceased friends, and even longer since I had seen Zasper. Some I hadn't even seen since coming out of the ice, Raven Bone being ever the recluse and Kasabian busy governing his territory. So I decided to have a gathering and invited a plethora of people for dinner.

I was busy preparing for their arrival, although some would return to their homes afterwards, others were spending the night at the palace before making the trip back. I checked on the menu and cooking, although I wasn't the best at making food I was an excellent consumer of it. And then there were the guest rooms that needed readying on top of all the other daily responsibilities of being a ruler. I did have to take a nap before they arrived in order to replenish my energy and hopefully rid myself of my headache.

Sleeping had revitalized me enough to greet my friends, and I was excited to spend time together with those who I had become inexplicably bonded with. Raven Bone came early to check on me, and I enjoyed talking with him. Although his blindness never caused him any physical pain, it was still a hindrance, still made his life more difficult than others, something I now could understand in a new, personal way.

The sacrifices were not always our lives; sometimes something unseen was taken instead. Dying, what so many deem the ultimate act of sacrifice, was, dare I say, easier than living broken, mourning what was lost.

Kalosa had declined to come, on account that only I would be able to understand her, but she sent her regards via Dryden and was happy to hear that I was doing better.

The new queen of the northern territory, Laika, had one hand propping her head while the other danced dangerously close to Raven Bone's.

The chief smiled wide, his skin almost the same color of his teeth. "Now Racour has two beautiful queens," he drawled as he reached over and pressed his lips to her hand.

Laika's face reddened, accentuating her blue eyes. "I heard from Her Majesty that you are blind, so such compliments seem shallow."

Raven Bone pulled out a stretch of cloth and began tying it around his head. "I guess there is no need to pretend then."

As his fingers fumbled trying to tie the cloth, Laika lifted her hands and said, "Allow me."

Raven Bone leaned towards her, the pleasure painted so obviously on his face. Shaking my head as I smiled, I turned my attention to the others.

The other kings were present as well, and King Koodsin had brought his dear sisters, who had thanked me for rescuing them. King Koodsin was still quiet, but he looked far happier, his face lighter than before. King Minsol was an awkward conversationalist, but he meant well and was loyal. His attempts at making conversation with Koodsin's sisters were met with deadly glares by their brother.

King Peten was also here with his mother, who had chosen to remain in Gwanji to expand her fabric business. She was discussing the pros and cons of certain fabrics with Larkan—Laika's brother—and he promised to visit her shop to pick fabrics for his tailoring business. Peten was enraptured by the dragons, and they were equally interested in him, although that was due to the meat he kept tossing up into the air for them to catch.

Kas was… Kas. He had brought his betrothed with him, something that had surprised us all. She was a tanned woman with short black hair and matching black ink crawling up one arm, and an almond shaped eye, the other one gone and covered with a patch—lost in a brutal fight in which she was the sole person to walk away although neither her nor Kas shared the circumstances of the brawl. She seemed rather serious for someone like Kasabian, but as he prattled on and compared her to every flower in the world, the corners of her lips turned up. I grabbed Lux's hand. Fire and ice could make a good combination.

Falchor had brought his wife and son to the palace, and little Draque, a patch of brown hair growing on his head like dry grass, was particularly fascinated with a flappy piece of cabbage that flung juice as he waved it around. Next to them was the Jang family, who had graciously accepted the invitation to join us. Citadel and Jun were discussing horses, while Hyesun and Ari talked about the ups and downs of motherhood. Minyoung had enticed

Dryden over by offering him a juicy chunk of duck, and he even allowed her to run her fingers through his pelt.

I offered them a house in the city, but they had declined, desiring to stay at their quaint farm. They had accepted the annual allowance though, and I promised that they were always welcome to ask for more but doubted they would.

Zenith's mother, along with Mordris' family, had declined to come, the grief still too much to bear, but sent their thanks. Ferrum and Talom had both resigned from their positions, likely at the insistence of their mother who had already lost a brother and husband to fighting. Zenith's mother had also sent an apology to Lux.

As we sat, ate and chatted, I noticed Lux picking out the mushrooms from the sweet potato noodles, piling them all to one side of his plate. Lifting his dish and leaning towards me, he plopped all the noodles on to my own, careful as to not allow the mushrooms to fall. I peered up at him, my lips curling upwards.

"When did you—"

He interrupted, shrugging, "I've observed more than you realize, my love."

And through the entire night, he was attentive, not only to me but to the others as well. When someone ran out of water, he poured them some himself, or when someone was looking for a dish, he would follow their gaze and pass them the plate.

My hand never left his leg, my fingers resting atop his knee.

I wished to do the same for him, to memorize his likes and dislikes, but with the brain frog, it was difficult to recall such details. However, Lux never minded, always the patient one out of the two of us.

Later that evening, Lux and I were sitting on the balcony, Bahm and Sol laying at his feet and Dryden at mine.

It was hard to swallow one's pride. The common folk would continue on, harvesting their fields and trading at the local shops, and even the other nations' courts would continue in their political bickering and gossip, none of them knowing how close they had been to disaster and destruction. They would offer no thanks or know of the great sacrifice that it took to defeat the darkness. They would continue on while we would be forever changed, the damage imprinted and the scars forever bearing witness to our loss. There was no glory despite what was given up.

I turned my head, eyes gazing over Lux, who was soaking in the last rays of the sun, expression relaxed and the tips of a smile tugging at his lips. Then I looked down where Dryden lay on his side, his tongue hanging out ever so slightly, and curled into his belly was a three-legged dragon whose own tongue mimicked that of the ice leopard's, dangling out of his mouth. Peering down at my lap, my fingers absentmindedly ran across emerald scales and grassy fur, Sol's tongue flicking in and out as she lay contently on my legs. My other hand reached out and grabbed Lux's scarred one, fingers intertwining. Smiling and eyes reflecting the sun's brilliant rays, they appeared almost violet.

"Is something the matter, Little Bird?" he asked, eyes scanning my face for any indication of my thoughts.

My lips curled into a smile, and my chest warmed. "No, my love, nothing is wrong. I'm just thankful for what we have."

His grin widened even further, and he leaned forward, giving me a peck on my lips. He relaxed back into his chair, shoulders slumping into the cushions.

I looked out over the balcony, savoring the pink and purple that tangled with the yellows and oranges in a dance in the sky. There was nothing that could replace those who had died or the dreams and health that were destroyed, but there was hope, a future. That future would have its own trials and tribulations, but it would not be the end. No. The end was an eternity of peace and reuniting with those who had gone ahead, and even though the path to that end would be lined with tears, it was a worthy goal and more glorious than anything in this life.

I would have to delegate more now, have to let go of my capabilities and expectations from before, since I could not handle everything by myself and had limited energy for each day. I did my best to be thankful, that at least I had caring people around me.

Every once in a while I would cry, the sorrow springing up randomly as I mourned all that I had lost, all that would never be now that this was me. I still didn't know why He didn't heal me, why I, and so many, were allowed to suffer, but that was faith I suppose—trusting His character while not knowing the why. It wasn't easy, but it was possible. As I waited expectantly for the day when I would go to Paradise, the day when the pain would cease, I would live the best I could, rule the best I could. With Lux by my side, life felt a little more tolerable.

I smiled at the sky, at The Creator who watched from above.

EPILOGUE

That was a terrible story. *Not enough me in it,* Dryden grumbled from where he laid on the floor.

"That's because it's *my* story," I retorted with a chuckle.

Dryden's ears flattened, and his head drooped. *Does that mean I am not important to you?*

I smiled, reaching out a hand to scratch his muzzle—always careful to avoid the ears. "If I write a sequel, I promise you will be in it more."

Dryden purred and rubbed his head against my blanket-covered legs.

"Mama!"

My head jerked towards the sound as Nabi came running with red cheeks, Taeho trailing behind her.

Nabi scrambled onto my lap, huffing and brow furrowed, and I could tell by her face that she was about to dive into a lengthy complaint of something her brother had done.

The words spilled from her mouth as Taeho stood indignantly next to Dryden. "Mama, Taeho told me that shadow people will come take me at night if I don't listen to my big brother." Her hands gripped my arm and her lower lip trembled as her anger turned to fear.

I kissed her forehead. "Don't worry, sweetie. You know your daddy will scare the shadow people away with his fire.

Besides, Uncle Raven has shadow magic, and you love it when he comes to visit."

Nabi contemplated my words for a moment before her mouth turned up in a smile. "And Dryden will eat the bad guys, right?" She paused, turning to look at the big cat.

Dryden shifted, his posture straightening. *Of course. I will always be there to protect you both.*

Nabi sighed as she asked, "Both? Taeho is a big meanie. He can take care of himself." She stuck her tongue out at her brother, who rolled his eyes and crossed his arms.

It came as a great shock to us that Nabi could hear Dryden, as she had no connection to the Polaris line that we knew of. However, whatever magical bond that belonged to the High Queens had passed on to her the moment I named her the heir.

"Alright, alright. Be nice to your brother, Nabi." I looked to Taeho and instructed, "And don't scare your little sister."

Taeho muttered something under his breath, and I was about to ask him to repeat what he said when his father entered.

Lux sauntered into the room, hands behind his back, eliciting excited squeals from the children.

Nabi bounced up and down on my lap, and my legs protested, my muscles sore from... well they were always sore. I smiled through the discomfort and asked, "What are you hiding? Do I smell—"

"Blackberry tarts!" The children and I shouted in unison as Lux revealed what was in his hands. Nabi slipped off my lap, charging towards the plate filled with the warm pastries. The children bounced up and down, smiles plastered on their faces.

Lux laughed and lowered the plate so they could grab a tart, and black goo streaked their cheeks and chins as they devoured the sweet treats.

Lux walked over to where I sat and planted a soft kiss on my head. "And how is my Little Bird today?" he asked, eyes scanning me for any signs of deception.

I smiled half-heartedly. "In pain, as usual."

He kneeled next to me. "What hurts the worst today?"

I lowered my gaze. "My knee. You know my legs always seem to hurt worse as the weather gets colder."

He frowned, his free hand reaching for my right leg, and he started massaging it. I stared at him, hoping he could see the gratitude and love in my eyes. He must have, as he leaned up to kiss my lips.

"Ew. Gross," Taeho muttered.

Nabi paid no mind as she was too busy laughing as Dryden licked the tart filling from her face.

My heart warmed, and I whispered a prayer of thanks to The Creator. I had gained things I would have never had had I not gotten ill, such as Taeho and Nabi, two orphans whose parents had died during a sudden outbreak of disease in Roh territory. It had only been two years since we had adopted them, and had I not been sick and been able to have offspring of my own, then I would have never been blessed with my children.

Taeho tilted his head and approached us. He pointed to the papers on my lap and asked, "What's that, mama?"

My fingers grazed the parchment imported from Percia. "It's a story."

"Can you read it to us?"

I shook my head and spoke gently, "No. Not yet. Maybe when you and your sister are older."

Taeho puffed out his chest and insisted, "I am old enough."

Lux smiled mischievously. "Oh yeah? Can you beat me in a fight?"

Taeho nodded, chin jutting into the air and hands curled into tiny fists.

Lux set the empty plate on the floor, shifted into a crouch and pounced on him, lifting the boy into the air and swinging him around. Taeho's laugh echoed in the room, melding with Nabi's giggles as Dryden tickled her with his whiskers.

A warmth slithered up my legs, and I pulled the blanket back. Sol and Bahm were untangling themselves as they woke from their nap. Sol scurried out from behind my legs and stretched next to my chair, but Bahm attempted to climb up into my lap. It was hard for him with only three legs, so I leaned down and plucked him from my feet. Their horns had sprouted. They had gotten bigger too, and in a few years they'd overtake Dryden. But they were not so big that I couldn't hold them, well, as long as I was sitting. I wasn't as strong as I used to be, could hardly use weapons, my magic the only thing seeming to be unaffected by my illness.

But it was enough.

This life was enough.

I was enough, even in my weakened state.

Bahm snuggled into my arms as we watched the others play. I felt pressure against my leg, and as I looked down I smiled, Sol having scooted closer, leaning against me.

I turned my head back up to see Lux, Taeho, Nabi, and Dryden in one heaping bundle on the floor. They were all struggling to breathe from too much laughter and the weight of the others pressing on them.

I whispered to the heavens, *Thank you.*

KASABIAN

ACKNOWLEDGEMENTS

Thank you to my parents who take care of me and my husband who holds me. Thank you to all who cheered me on.

A special thanks to Ashley, for jumping out of fridges for me, and for Seth, our pirate captain and cheerleader. To Kate, who always comments on my posts and shares them, and to C.K. for always lifting others up.

This book would have been a complete disaster if not for my amazing beta readers: Manda, Ruby G. (this period is supposed to be there I promise), and Alexus. They edited this book and pushed me to revise it in the best ways. You have them to thank for more environmental descriptions.

Most importantly, to my Creator, who although has not healed me, has bestowed upon me many blessings. Much like Valine, I don't understand *why*, but I trust that He will use my pain for a purpose.

Lastly to my readers, thank you. Thank you for the kind messages that help keep me writing. Thank you for taking the time to read this book and following along Valine and co.'s journey. I hope they can make you feel a little less alone on your own journey.

여보,
오빠를 생각하면서 럭스 썼다.
오빠는 내 꿈, 내 희망이다.
나 울때 안아주고 아플때 마사지 해주니까 너무 고
맙고 우리 늙게 돼도 사랑할거야.

OTHER BEX GIL BOOKS

Completed Duology:
Throne of Anguish
Crown of Sorrows

Stand Alone:
Daughters of the Sun *(Novella-August 2024)*
Bound to the Tyrant King *(Winter 2024)*